Something or someone dashed across Carys's headlights. Panic gripped her as a male figure came toward her side of the vehicle, moving directly at her.

She reached for anything she could use as a weapon and double-checked that she'd locked the doors.

With nothing to defend herself with, she and the baby would be at the mercy of anyone who got inside the vehicle with them.

Carys recited a silent protection prayer and hoped like hell it would be enough to keep them safe. And then she remembered where she was and what she had. She fumbled for her phone, then managed to tap the most recent call.

The second Blaize answered, she said, "Help!"

"Where are you?" he asked.

"No idea," she said. "I was on my way to your ranch and turned off onto a gravel farm road after the highway."

A loud crack sounded. She screamed.

The call dropped.

CUSTODY IN THE CROSSHAIRS

BARB HAN

INTRIGUE

All my love to Brandon, Jacob and Tori, my three greatest loves.

To Babe, my hero, for being my best friend, my greatest love and my place to call home. I love you with everything that I am.

And to all the readers who are on this journey with me. I am eternally grateful for you!

Recycling programs for this product may not exist in your area.

ISBN-13: 978-1-335-18907-3

Custody in the Crosshairs

Harlequin Enterprises ULC
22 Adelaide St. West, 41st Floor
Toronto, Ontario M5H 4E3, Canada
www.Harlequin.com

HarperCollins Publishers
Macken House, 39/40 Mayor Street Upper,
Dublin 1, D01 C9W8, Ireland
www.HarperCollins.com

Printed in Lithuania

1 2 3 4 5 6 7 8 9 10 LIT 28 27 26 25

USA TODAY bestselling author **Barb Han** lives in north Texas with her very own hero-worthy husband, three beautiful children, a spunky golden retriever/standard poodle mix and too many books in her to-read pile. In her downtime, she plays video games and spends much of her time on or around a basketball court. She loves interacting with readers and is grateful for their support. You can reach her at barbhan.com.

Books by Barb Han

Harlequin Intrigue

Wilde Country

Custody in the Crosshairs

Marshals of Mesa Point

Ranch Ambush
Bounty Hunted
Captured in West Texas
Escape: Big Bend Canyon
Lone Star Country Protector
Twin Threats in Austin

The Cowboys of Cider Creek

Rescued by the Rancher
Riding Shotgun
Trapped in Texas
Texas Scandal
Trouble in Texas
Murder in Texas

Visit the Author Profile page at Harlequin.com.

CAST OF CHARACTERS

Blaize Wilde—He inherits a crumbling Texas ranch—and an unexpected mystery in the form of baby Lark.

Carys Aldric—A young Child Protective Services agent with fierce moral courage and a heart too big for her role's boundaries.

Lark Wilde—A three-month-old infant at the center of a dangerous mystery.

Stephanie Cross—Mysterious mother of Lark, believed to be deceased.

Leah Mendez—Guarded, anxious neighbor of Stephanie's.

Kit—Grandmother who stands to lose her home.

Silus Vexler—Small-time crime boss on the hunt for Stephanie.

Chapter One

Blaize Wilde walked outside the broken-down barn at Wilde Cattle Ranch taking mental inventory of the shitshow he and his two brothers had just inherited. The weathered wood planks and rusted metal roofing sheets with pieces missing wouldn't be complete without peeling paint and cracked walls. How was he supposed to get this place up and running without a bank load of cash?

"No one would blame you for selling to get what you can out of it." Kit, his grandmother, ambled up, catching him off guard while he'd been deep in thought.

You would. Kit had built this small cattle ranch with Blaize's grandfather. Her son had drained the place of money and spirit. Selling now meant his beloved grandmother would have to move from the only home she'd known for more than fifty years. Not happening. Period.

"There's work to be done to get the place back in shape." Blaize stood in front of a barn in need of far more than a coat of paint. It could use a torch. Starting from the ground up might be easier than attempting to salvage what was left of this rickety old, neglected building. "Nothing we can't handle."

He forced a smile.

"Have you found your brothers yet?" Kit asked, slipping her bony fingers through the crook in his arm and then holding on to him like she needed him for balance.

"No, ma'am."

"Well, you got the news about your father's passing last night and showed up before the sun," she said. "You should try to get some rest after driving all night." Blue eyes stared up at him, still bright.

"I'm good."

Cormac's death was no loss to the world. A few liquor manufacturers might feel the drop in sales, though. When your last name was Wilde, the jokes wrote themselves. They also got old real quick. Cormac did his best to live up to the family name. His sons couldn't stand the man for it.

Blaize glanced down into serious eyes framed by wrinkled skin.

"How are you doing with it all, by the way?" She waved her free hand like she was presenting paradise, but the twinge of sadness mixed with helplessness in her gaze told the real story. She was afraid for her future. Yet she would never put pressure on the grandsons she loved.

"Me? Like I said, I'm fine." Cormac had never been much of a father. The irony there being Blaize had wanted the whole wife-and-kids package, figuring he could do better than his father. "The world is better off without a person like Cormac in it, as far as I'm concerned."

Another glance told him that he'd struck a raw nerve.

"I'm sorry, Kit. I didn't mean to say your son was a—"

She clucked her tongue, stopping him mid-sentence. "Nonsense. There's nothing to apologize for." She squeezed his arm. "He gave me three incredible grandchildren. It might have been asking too much for him to be good, too."

Three grandchildren from three different mothers, married to none. Cormac was a real piece of work. Kit had hinted there was a time when he wasn't like that. As far as Blaize was concerned, there was no excuse good enough to cover the man's lies and reckless behavior.

"Thank you, by the way," he said, wanting to change the subject. He smiled and patted her hand. "I'm pretty sure you just gave me a compliment."

"I meant every word." She looked up at him with a devilish grin. "I'd keep throwing out compliments, but you'll accuse me of brown-nosing to keep my bedroom at the ranch."

Blaize laughed for the first time in a very long time.

"You don't have to worry about being evicted as long as I'm around." He wanted to offer reassurance even though he couldn't be certain his brothers would agree to keeping the place. If he could locate them. Since neither were on social media, preferring to stay off the grid, he was limited as to how he could reach his brothers. All he had was phone numbers, no addresses.

"Speaking of you boys, did you get a hold of Raiden or Phoenix?"

He shook his head.

"They'll turn up," she said. "They always do."

"I'd settle for them answering my calls."

Not that they had a reason to. Blaize had been living in his own hell for the past couple of years. Losing the person you promised to spend the rest of your life with had a way of obliterating every piece of you and causing you to go dark with everyone you knew or cared about. Your world shrank. You cut people out of your life. Lashed out. Blaize couldn't blame his brothers for not answering his calls or texts anymore. He'd been a jerk to them, and they had no idea why.

"They will," Kit said, turning toward the farmhouse that was in almost as bad a shape as the barn. "But first, what should I cook for dinner? Something nice to celebrate your homecoming."

"Don't go to any trouble on my account."

She batted her free hand at him playfully. "You coming home qualifies as special, Blaize."

"Fine." He knew better than to start an argument with Kit despite some of her spark dimming with every passing year. There was enough flicker there to light a fire when provoked. "A special occasion calls for steaks on the grill."

"Now you're talking," she said as her eyes lit up. "The corn on the cob at Harden's stand up the road is the best. We'll pick up some of that along with a pair of potatoes. We can do 'em up with sour cream and the works."

"It'll be a feast."

Blaize liked the excitement in her eyes and the hope in her voice.

The cattle ranch was in dire straits. He'd stayed up part of the night driving and the rest looking into the books. He hoped like hell he didn't let her down the way he'd disappointed his wife. *Former wife.* The reality of those words struck like a physical blow. Blaize was no longer married. He was thirty-five years old. No kids. Very little money. And now he needed to save this small cattle ranch or watch his grandmother lose her home.

Life sure as hell knew how to kick you in the teeth when you were down.

Gloomy gray clouds rolled overhead. A couple of rain drops splatted on his forehead. Lightning streaked across an ever-darkening sky. Thunder boomed a few seconds later.

He ducked his head down. "We better head inside before this gets worse."

In Blaize's life, it always did.

Carys Holmes held a three-month-old baby in her arms, gently bouncing up and down in a feeble attempt to stop the little girl from crying. *Hopeless.* Carys was hopeless. This attempt was hopeless.

In times like these, she seriously questioned her career choice. Holding an inconsolable baby definitely fit into the downside category.

Her office door opened. Harrison Tucker poked his head inside.

“What is that baby still doing here?” her coworker asked, frowning, practically yelling over the noise.

It didn’t help. The little one screamed louder.

“I think she’s sick.”

He stared at her like *...And?*

“It’s just hard to throw her in a car seat and then drop her off at an orphanage when she’s this upset.”

The air stilled as the baby sucked in a breath before launching another ear-splitting wail. The kid had a good set of lungs on her.

“That’s the job, sweetheart.” The frown lines on Harrison’s face softened.

“She’s a baby, Harrison. Sister’s Love is severely understaffed right now. They had two people quit last week alone.” Carys looked down at the baby, who was winding up to belt out another loud cry. “They won’t have time to hold her like this.”

He pursed his lips. “Some days, this job is the worst and you go home wondering if you made any difference at all. Other days, you see a once-troubled teen now making straight A’s in school and on a better path because you intervened and they listened to your advice.”

That still didn’t answer the question of how she was supposed to drop off an innocent child at an understaffed orphanage. There were no available foster families and her babysitter's husband said the baby couldn't stay with them.

"She's already lost so much already," Carys said. "And there's at least some hope the woman the vehicle was registered to had loaned out her car. It is possible the baby's mother wasn't the one driving." The fiery crash made it difficult to positively ID the female driver.

"There's no proof she wasn't, either. And the mother hasn't shown up, so she still needs to be taken in."

Fair point. Carys didn't have a comeback for that.

The baby belted out another shrill. Did she know her mother might be gone? *Is gone, Carys. There's no reason to hold out hope the mother is somehow still alive.*

"Sorry about knocking, but I have a raging headache and these walls are paper thin," Harrison said as soon as she sucked in a breath.

"I have aspirin in the top drawer if you'd like some." Carys needed to figure out a plan to quiet the crying. Her heart was cracking in half at the pitiful sounds—sounds that she could relate to for the same soul-deep reason. Loss.

He shook his head. "Took some a few minutes ago." He paused for a beat, resigned. "You'll locate and notify the father or a family member, and she'll be picked up in no time. She might not even spend the night at Sister's. You know how that goes." He squinted like it hurt to look at anyone. "Plus, it's Friday and you probably have a hot date tonight."

Everything he said made sense, except the last part.

She almost laughed. Instead, she cracked a smile. "You know it."

"Wait. I was kidding. You do?" His face scrunched. More pain?

"No. Nothing." His reaction caught her off guard. It was likely the pain of his headache causing his face to twist with concern when he believed she had a date. Why would he care?

She chalked it up to curiosity and nothing more.

At twenty-four years old, she'd been on the job for two, going on three, years following college graduation. Harrison had worked here for six. Clearly he had more experience—and was probably right.

"We can't wear a red cape for everyone who comes through the front door, Carys." With those words, he waved and closed her door.

He might have had more time on the job, but that didn't mean he had as much compassion. Did those extra three years harden him?

Harrison would agree—this job was difficult. You were exposed to child abuse and neglect that made you lose faith in humanity. Carys decided on day one of the job that when the bad days outnumbered the good, it would be time to move on. While she was occupying this desk, however, she would do everything in her power to help kids and families.

Did that mean bending a few rules when necessary?

Carys gently placed the baby in her carrier seat, then strapped her in.

Phone. Wallet. Keys.

Once Carys had all three, she grabbed the carrier's handle and then headed out of the office. Taking the baby to her nearby rented two-bedroom bungalow wasn't a big deal. Her home was warmer than this sterile office environment. Two years on the job already, and Carys had yet to make the space hers. There were no pictures sitting on her desk. Nothing personal on the walls.

No wonder the little girl couldn't get comfortable.

After securing the carrier in the back seat, Carys made the short drive. Halfway there, the little one quieted.

"Do you like car rides?" Carys whispered. She should have thought of the move earlier. It would have saved her ears and the baby's lungs. She glanced at the rearview mirror. The girl's face was still red. Her forehead had been warm earlier. Carys couldn't decide if the baby was sick or just overheated.

She pulled the sedan onto the parking pad next to her house and then cut the engine. She took a deep breath and waited a few seconds for the screaming to kick up again.

It was quiet.

A small win. Carys was more convinced than ever that she'd made the right call in taking the baby out of the office. The office kept a loose work-from-home policy following the pandemic, so her absence shouldn't raise any alarm bells. Her boss might even think Carys was on her way to the orphanage. Good. That could buy more time. She could reach out to the director, Rosie Baumgarten, after lunch.

As a bonus, now that there was peace, Carys could log into the work computer via her laptop and take a deeper look at the baby's file. Locating next of kin before the workday ended was her primary focus before she had to drop off the little girl at the orphanage. The little one had stayed overnight at her babysitter's house and the change in routine had probably added to her fussiness.

After taking the carrier inside and setting up at the kitchen table, she made a cup of coffee and checked the time. Eleven thirty. Good. She had plenty of daylight hours left to locate next of kin once she looked up the birth certificate.

Storm clouds had rolled in on the way home. Rain splatted against the windows.

Thankfully, Ruby Lark was still out. She must be exhausted.

Carys wondered if the baby girl was called Ruby, Rue, or Lark. Then again, it wouldn't surprise her if she was called by her full name, Ruby Lark. This was Texas. Two names weren't out of the question. Since Carys had always liked the name Rue for a nickname, she decided to go with that one for the time being.

Fingers tapping on the keyboard, she glanced at the intake form. There wasn't much there she didn't already know.

The vehicle owner's name was Stephanie Cross. The deputy on scene's name was Levi Liu. Carys made a mental note of the names as she skimmed down the page. There wasn't much else.

Huh.

Thankfully she'd requested a court order to give her access to the child's birth certificate before taking custody of Rue. The permission should be granted before end of day if all went well.

What was she supposed to do until then?

She tapped her fingers against the table, waited.

An hour passed by while getting caught up on paperwork from other cases. Then another.

Her stomach growled.

As she reached toward the laptop to close it down, an update dinged. The permission to access Rue's birth certificate came through. Curiosity got the best of her, so she immediately accessed the TxEVER system, a secure database, and got a name.

Blaize Wilde. She rolled her eyes. *Now that sounds like a stable person.*

Taking note that the last names didn't match, Carys located his cell number and made the call, hearing the first ring and waiting for voicemail to click in. No one ever picked up calls from strangers.

"Hello?" Blaize's deep masculine voice caused a visceral reaction in her body.

"Mr. Wilde?"

"Speaking."

Carys mentally shook off the shock of hearing his voice. "My name is Carys. I'm afraid I have bad news. Are you sitting down?"

"Don't need to," he said on a loaded sigh. "Go ahead and get it over with. Tell me the reason you called."

"I work with Child Protective Services, and your daughter, Ruby Lark Wilde, is in my custody."

"Excuse me?" The degree of shock in his voice said this was likely the first time he was being told about his daughter. And now he was going to have to learn someone he cared about might be dead.

"My apologies if this is the first—"

"You have the wrong person," he said. "I never fathered a child."

"Your name is listed on the birth certificate, Mr. Wilde. And I'm quite certain that—"

"Sounds like someone has been drinking from the outside hose too long," he said and then hung up.

What kind of irresponsible jerk fathered a child and then walked away, leaving the mother to raise a child on her own?

That bastard.

He was also Rue's only hope of not being turned over to an orphanage tonight since there was no other next of kin to be found.

Biting back a slew of curses, Carys tapped the phone

icon on her screen. She hit *Recents*, tapped the number at the top of her screen, and clamped her mouth closed.

When he answered this time, he would get an earful. The call rolled to voicemail. *Of course it did.*

"Listen here, you total piece of…" She took in a deep breath, reminding herself that she was leaving a recorded message that could be used against her later. "I have a sick baby in my custody who needs her father to step up to the plate or she'll be left at an understaffed orphanage after losing the one parent who loved her enough to stick around." Realizing she'd gone too far, she ended the call and prayed those words wouldn't be the reason she was fired.

As she set the phone down, it buzzed.

He was calling back.

Chapter Two

"I just saw that you're leaving a message, so you might as well tell me what it says." Blaize barely got the words out before a grunt came through the line. It was quickly followed by an apology along with a plea to delete the voicemail without listening to it.

He said he would.

"Here's what I know so far—I have a baby girl in my custody who I'm about to be forced to take somewhere that won't be a good place for her right now, and you're the only parent I can locate."

"What happened to her mother?" He wasn't a jerk. He might not have the first clue how his name ended up on the kid's birth certificate, but he cared what happened on a basic human level.

"There was a car accident."

"Oh." He sat with that for a moment. "Hold on. You said that I'm the only parent you can locate. To be clear, the kid isn't mine. But what happened and how did you get my—"

"The car caught on fire, and the driver hasn't been positively ID'd as of yet and might not be for days. The car is registered to a woman named Stephanie Cross."

"And you're ready to get the little one in your custody out of your hair," he said.

"Did I say that?" The high-pitched shrill quality to her voice told him the degree to which he'd just messed up. This was bad. "No. I didn't. For your information, sir, I'd happily spend all the time necessary with this angel. However, I've already severely broken the rules by bringing her to my home and could end up fired, so there's that."

Blaize let her speak without interruption. "Carys. Is that your name?"

"Yes."

"You sound like a decent human being going out of your way to protect a child while putting your job on the line." The fact that she'd broken the rules said she cared more about doing what was right than staying employed. He applauded her for the move. Integrity like that didn't come around as often as it should.

"I'd like to think so," she said, some of the defensiveness eased from her tone.

"Here's my problem." He waited a couple of beats. "There's no possible way that I'm the father."

"Your name is on the birth certificate, sir."

"Call me Blaize. My name is Blaize."

"It won't make a difference what I call you," she said. "You're still the only name I have to work with."

He issued a sharp sigh. "Is there no other choice? Just me?"

"I can't find a list of next of kin for the mother, if that's what you're asking," she said. "These things can take time."

"You can release the baby to me if I agree?" How was that even possible?

"Yes."

"What's the mother's name again?"

"Stephanie Cross."

Blaize still drew a blank. "How old is this baby?"

"Three months," she said.

That young? What was he supposed to do with an infant?

Thunder boomed, shaking the house as he walked into the kitchen to get a drink of water. Sitting at the table nursing a cup of coffee was the answer. "Hold on a second, okay?"

"Sure," Carys said, drawing out the word.

He moved the phone from his ear and caught his grandmother's attention. "How are you with babies?"

Her eyebrows shot up. "Why do you ask?"

"A friend needs a sitter, possibly overnight, and I don't have the first clue as to how to take care of a kid."

She smiled. A tiny spark lit her eyes. "Are you asking for my help?"

"I guess I am."

"It's been a long time, but I imagine not too much has changed. They still take bottles and need diaper changes." She shrugged and widened the smile. "Might be nice to have a baby around, even if only for a short while."

"I'll owe you one big time."

She winked before taking a sip and making a production of setting the cup down. "I'll take you up on it someday."

They both knew she wouldn't. She never asked for anything, and he was beginning to see how much he'd neglected this place and her. Guilt punched him. Regret stabbed him in the chest. He might have reason to hate Cormac, but Blaize should have checked on his own grandmother more.

He was here now. He would do better.

Before he got the phone back to his ear, the loud baby cries overrode the thunder cracking outside.

"Carys?"

"You'll have to speak up," she said. "I can barely hear you."

"Should I come to you, or how should we do this?" He had no idea how any of this worked and couldn't be more outside his comfort zone. This baby might not belong to him, but offering a hand was the right thing to do. Call it residual guilt for not being able to save his own wife. He'd never felt more helpless during her long illness. This, he could do.

A voice in the back of his head said, *You were of no use then, and you'll be pointless now.* Choosing to ignore it and the knot tightening in his chest, he said, "I'm ready to do what I can to help."

"What? I'm sorry—I can't hear you."

He practically had to shout the words a second time.

"Send me your address," she said. "I'll come to you."

He agreed and then ended the call.

Kit clucked her tongue. "Is there something you need to tell me?"

"Funny story." He poured a cup of coffee and joined her at the table after texting the address to the ranch. "A person I've never heard of before put my name down on a birth certificate."

"What?" Kit's eyes saucers.

"I know. Strange, isn't it?" A crack of thunder rumbled in the distance. The storm was intensifying. So much for grilling outside.

"And you're sure you've never met the woman?"

"Not to my knowledge." He took a sip of coffee. "And I sure as hell didn't sleep around. Not with everything going on with…"

Blaize clamped his mouth shut.

Kit reached across the table and patted his hand. Her frail, bony fingers were small by comparison. "Of course, you don't owe me any explanations." She caught his gaze. "You know that, right?"

He nodded.

"I just wish you would talk about what happened with someone. Doesn't have to be me."

Rain battered the roof. A drip sounded behind him.

He bit back a curse as he pushed up to standing. "I'll keep that in mind. Right now, I need to fix a leak before we need swimsuits to be in this old house."

She opened her mouth to speak before clamping it shut again. "I'll get a bucket."

RAIN POUNDED THE front windshield to the point where the windshield wipers were essentially just decorations. Carys white-knuckled the steering wheel. The car ride seemed to upset the baby this time. Thunder boomed and lightning streaked the sky. Almost-black clouds rolled across the velvet canopy. No stars were out.

This was a bad omen.

Winds kicked up, shaking the sedan. Debris flew across the road in the form of branches and trash. An actual trash can slammed into the hood of her sedan, then bounced off. *We're not in Kansas anymore, Dorothy.*

The thought of a tornado ripping through the streets was enough to fry her last nerve. She was closer to the ranch than her home, so it made the most sense to keep going. Winds howled louder than the baby's cries.

This was not good. So not good.

I choose to be strong. She repeated the mantra that had gotten her through a few very rough years when she was younger, including surviving an overbearing father after her mother died.

She glanced in the rearview mirror at the red-faced baby.

"I understand what you're about to go through better than you realize, Rue. You aren't the only one who lost a mother before you could remember anything about her."

Carys didn't wish death on anyone. For Rue's sake, she hoped the driver wasn't Stephanie Cross. The odds were most definitely against it being the case, but she could hold on to the thought until proven otherwise.

Holding on to the steering wheel for dear life as winds pushed the vehicle around, she navigated onto the farm road leading to the ranch. Gravel spewed behind her tires as she pushed the vehicle to go faster.

Branches flew in front of the windshield. Being out here was dangerous. She should have asked Blaize to meet her at her home instead. What had she been thinking? *You weren't. You were in emergency mode.*

Carys repeated the mantra moments before slamming on the brakes. She careened sideways, narrowly missing a tree trunk.

Her first instinct was to hop out of the driver's side and comfort the child. The baby's loud cries said her lungs were still working as Carys slipped into the back seat. Rain pelted her face and torso. Her button-down shirt needed to be wrung out by the time she slammed the door shut behind her. Her second instinct was to lock the doors as the tiny hairs on the back of her neck pricked.

She glanced around, searching for signs of someone being out here. The feeling they weren't alone nearly overwhelmed her. A second later, she could have sworn a shadow passed by on the passenger side of the car.

An involutory shiver rocked her body as icy fingers gripped her spine. *I choose to be strong.*

Blowing out a calming breath, she refocused on the baby. The buckles on the car seat were not the easiest to navigate.

She noticed how shaky her own hands were as she tried to unclick the chest clip holding the straps in place.

"I'm sorry that I'm so bad at this, little Rue," she said, mustering as soothing a voice as she possibly could while under duress. "It'll be okay."

How many times had she wished her own father would have said those words to her while growing up? Instead, he'd overprotected her to the point of stifling her. He'd become obsessed with keeping her safe, which meant never letting her out of the house except for school and school-related activities. She'd joined pretty much every club in high school just to have an excuse to leave the house. He'd denied sleepover requests. *What if the girl has a brother who'd abuse you in the middle of the night or a father who has bad intentions?*

The closer college came, the more he bore down on her, making any kind of life impossible. By her senior year of high school, she'd had it.

I'm moving to campus, she'd said. *And there's nothing you can do to stop me.* It was the first time in her life that she'd stood up for herself and gone against him. Pushing back against the person who raised you—no matter how hard they'd made your life—was the hardest thing to do.

Then I'm not responsible for you had been his comeback.

True to his words, he cut her off financially. They'd had a huge dustup over the move, not because she was mad about the money. She could—and did!—take out loans to get through her four years of school. She'd worked double shifts and crashed on a friend's couch after the required first year of dorm living to save money.

Her father couldn't handle her independence. He threw every name in the book at her when she dug her heels in. He'd accused her of being a harlot—the nicer-sounding word for slut—even though she'd never had sex, let alone a boyfriend.

The fight, the horrible words he'd called her, caused her to lose her father more than the decision to leave did. Because she wanted nothing to do with him after the way he talked to her.

The wall that had come up between them had become impenetrable and strong as steel. She'd contacted him before graduation, humbled herself, and asked him to be there.

He never responded to her text, never showed.

Fine. She decided not to lose sleep over it. Her stubborn streak, it turned out, came from her father.

The car seat's chest clip finally opened. *Thank the stars for small miracles.*

Carys gently wrapped her hands around the little girl and lifted. The crying nearly broke Carys's heart.

"I'm here, little one," she soothed, bringing the baby toward her until the little girl was against Carys's chest. She looked down at the pitiful creature who was so upset. It struck her that Rue had a binky earlier. "Do you need your binky?" She managed to find it in the seat. The second the rubber tip touched the baby's cheek, she rooted for the comfort item.

It was then Carys realized the kid might be hungry.

At least the binky quieted the cries. A sense of satisfaction replaced the deep-seeded failure from moments ago.

Carys didn't want kids. Barely in her mid-twenties, she hardly wanted a boyfriend. Though, after the last one, she needed a minute to regroup. Jack had too many of her father's tendencies. After two months of dating, he wanted the password to her cell phone so he could check texts for her.

Like she needed a gatekeeper for her messages. His jealous streak turned ugly fast, and she couldn't move on quick enough. Weeks after the breakup, if you could even call it that since they'd never had a conversation about being in a relationship, he still showed up in the parking lot with flowers.

Then there was Leonard. He'd been older, which she'd assumed meant wiser. At almost forty, he'd been surprisingly less emotionally mature than some of the teens she worked with since taking the CPS job.

Suddenly, something or someone dashed across the headlights. Panic gripped Carys as a male figure came toward her side of the vehicle, moving directly at her.

She reached for anything she could use as a weapon and double-checked that she'd locked the doors.

With nothing to defend herself with, she and Rue would be at the mercy of anyone who got inside the vehicle with them.

Carys recited a silent protection prayer she'd learned in religious school as a kid and hoped like hell it would be enough to keep them safe. And then she remembered where she was and what she had. She fumbled her phone, then managed to tap the most recent call.

The second Blaize answered, she said, "Help!"

Chapter Three

The panic in Carys's voice against the backdrop of severe weather caused the stress knot to tighten in his chest. "Where are you?"

"No idea," she said.

Not at all helpful.

"I was on my way to your ranch and turned off onto a gravel farm road after the highway."

Better.

A loud crack sounded. She screamed.

The call dropped.

Back to not good.

Blaize turned toward the kitchen door. Kit stood there, blocking his exit.

"Where do you think you're going in this mess?" she asked. Her gaze shot to the set of keys hanging next to the door.

"I have to go." He started toward her.

She stepped aside. "In this? Be reasonable, Blaize. You could get hurt out there. You're no match for a storm this size."

Wind howled. A few seconds later, something substantial slammed against the side of the house as though punctuating her sentence. It was not lost on him that flying debris killed far too many people in weather like this.

"You could get hurt or worse, Blaize. I'm serious."

"Someone could die if I don't go," he said.

Kit gave a small nod. She, of all people, would understand his need to help someone in need. It was the ranching way, ingrained in all of them since birth. Somehow it had skipped a generation with Cormac, but that was another story.

"If you have to do this, be careful out there," Kit said, a worry wrinkle adding to the ones already scoring her forehead.

"You know I will."

With that, he grabbed the keys to his old Jeep and headed out the door. The second he stepped outside rain pelted him like BBs. He tucked his chin to his chest and made a beeline to his Jeep that was parked on the pad next to the one-story ranch-style house.

Once inside, he claimed the driver's seat and started the ignition. The Jeep would fare better than other types of vehicles in this mess of a storm. Texas weather in the spring was as unpredictable as serious illness. Some folks' DNA was a ticking time bomb that, once unleashed, could get out of control fast. At least, that had been the case for Lynn. She'd gone from being the most alive person he'd ever met to sick and sicker in a matter of months.

Storms like this one always reminded him of Lynn. She'd left this world, and him, on a night much like this one.

He navigated down the lane and toward the farm road, face wet with a mix of rain and hot tears—tears that had taken too long to fall. They burned as they rolled down his cheek and dripped onto his shirt. Blaize never wanted to feel that helpless again in this lifetime. An image of Lynn stamped his thoughts. Not sick, almost-dying Lynn. But the one he'd fallen head over heels for.

A thump on the side of the Jeep cleared every distraction, bringing his focus back to the stretch of road in front of him.

Potholes on the lane had him bouncing around, but he didn't care. He needed to get to Carys and the baby girl.

Trying to call back did no good as he was being tossed around like a fishing boat in a storm and he'd lost cell coverage. He muttered a few choice words under his breath as he navigated toward the spot he was certain Carys was stuck.

Barreling down the lane, he turned onto the farm road. Panic struck, causing the stress knot to tighten even more. He had no idea if her vehicle had been struck or if she'd had to abandon it altogether.

The thought of her stuck outside with no shelter sat hard on his chest. Add an infant into the equation and the boulder on his chest dug in deeper. Mud kicked up, splattering on the windows. The windshield wipers couldn't keep up with the barrage.

It had been a long time since he'd been on this road. Muscle memory kicked in as he gripped the steering wheel with both hands. He should be coming up on the spot he believed Carys to be stranded.

Stranded and in trouble—a dangerous combination.

LIGHTING SHOT ACROSS the sky. Carys strained to get a good look out the driver's-side window. A figure, dressed in all black with a hoodie over their head, stood tall. Arms raised, Carys couldn't tell what the person was holding, but it seemed obvious what they were about to do.

An object landed with a thud against the pane. A crack?

The phone had slipped from Carys's hand while she'd been trying to maneuver the child back into the carrier. She muttered a curse as she felt around on the floorboard for the device while keeping one hand on Rue. She calmed with physical contact and a binky. Since Carys had no way to heat a bottle and no idea if the baby could drink formula cold, she needed to do whatever she could to keep the child calm until she could be turned over to her father.

Another thud snapped her back to the person trying to break into the vehicle. Carys had never felt more defenseless in her life. If it was just her, she could slip out the passenger-side door and run for her life. She might not be considered tall, but she could run. Running was one of the extra curriculars that got her out of the house at five o'clock in the morning during the school year when home had become a prison.

Headlights bounced up and down. The hooded figure ran off and disappeared.

A Jeep roared up next to her vehicle. A substantial male immediately jumped out of the driver's side. This had to be Blaize. For one, he came from the correct direction. Who else would be out here in this mess? The man made a beeline toward her.

Carys unlocked the door as the baby stirred.

He opened it but didn't make a move to get inside. After introducing himself, he said, "Let's get you two moved into my Jeep."

"Okay," she said, setting the baby in the carrier before handing her over to Blaize. She glanced around as she unhooked the base. "But someone was trying to break into my vehicle, so be careful."

"What the hell?" he asked as he took the carrier and then immediately got the baby inside the Jeep with Carys's help.

Next, he shielded Carys as she exited her sedan after clumsily grabbing her purse and locating her cell on the floor.

He stood next to her while she secured the base. She immediately climbed into the back seat after shouldering the diaper bag and grabbed the carrier once settled.

She scanned the area, but it was pitch black outside, way too dark to see anything. The occasional lightning bolt lit up the sky, but not long enough to see anything clearly. This area was rural, and trees lined the farm road.

"Thank you for coming out in this," she said to Blaize as he took the driver's seat. She could only imagine what he must've thought of her. She was supposed to take care of Rue, not place the little girl in harm's way even further. "I should have stayed home to ride it out."

He waved her off like it was nothing as he banked a U-turn back toward his ranch. "You were acting in the best interest of the kid."

"Was I? Bringing her out in this?" She was still shaking from the encounter with the person intent on harming them. "Not to mention the person who…"

An involuntary shiver rocked her body.

"Speaking of that, did you get a description?" He had to raise his voice to speak over the thunder booms.

Rue spit out her binky and started crying.

"That might be the most pitiful sound I've ever heard in my life," Blaize said, glancing at them through the rearview mirror.

He had the most interesting shade of blue-green eyes she'd ever seen. They were like staring into deep turquoise pools. After standing next to him, she knew he had to be at least six feet two inches, maybe a little more. He had a substantial build. Carys told herself she only noticed because of the threat of danger a few moments ago. On a basic, biological level, she needed to know he could protect her while she was vulnerable. Being with a baby had never made her feel more helpless. You couldn't run from danger while finagling an infant in your arms. You couldn't fight back. She felt defenseless.

Carys had a new understanding and a whole new respect for what mothers must go through on a daily basis. She didn't mean in the physical danger sense because what had just happened was rare. Trying to protect something so tiny and fragile, despite the lung capacity, would be a full-time job.

The baby kept up the crying as they pulled beside a ranch-style farmhouse that looked severely in need of TLC. Part of her job was to evaluate environments and people. She'd been a CPS worker for the past two years. Enough time to get a feel for people and places within a few minutes of meeting them or entering their space.

Blaize over the phone caused a lot of alarm bells to sound. She gave him grace for the fact he was finding out that he was a father from a stranger—not exactly an ideal situation. He claimed there was no possible way he fathered Rue. She needed to have a conversation with him about that before leaving her with him.

But first. Quiet the baby. Then? Coffee.

"What can I do to help?" Blaize asked as he pulled the lever that made the driver's seat go up so she could exit the Jeep.

"Take her," she said, handing over the carrier once more. Carys climbed out of the back seat and rushed toward the back door a half step behind Blaize. He stopped a little too suddenly, causing her to walk right into his back—a very muscled, brick-wall-type back. "Sorry."

If he noticed, he didn't say a word. Instead, he opened the door for her and ushered her inside.

Water dripped into a bucket a foot away from the fridge. The place was old and small but tidy.

A grandmotherly figure hopped up from her spot at the kitchen table, eyes as bright as her smile. "I can heat up water in the kettle."

"That would be amazing," Carys said. "Thank you."

The older woman practically beamed. "Call me Kit."

"I'm Carys."

Blaize set the baby carrier on top of the kitchen table, away from the *splunk* sounds coming from the bucket.

With all three of them working, Rue had a bottle in her mouth, happily sucking the milk within a matter of minutes with Kit doing the honors.

Carys cornered Blaize near the sink. "Thank you for rescuing us, by the way."

"Don't mention it." He issued a sharp sigh. "I'm concerned about the person on the loose who attacked your vehicle. You're sure they were trying to get to you?"

"What other option is there?"

"I don't know." He shrugged massive shoulders. "Maybe they thought you were trapped and couldn't unlock the door?"

She was already shaking her head before he could finish that sentence. "I was in plain sight."

"But you didn't get a description of them?"

"Not with the dark clothing and hoodie they were wearing."

"Male or female?"

"It was impossible to tell." Frustrating as hell, too. "It was dark, and they were wearing oversized clothing that basically made it impossible to make out any shapes other than a general description of, like, they were a human being."

She issued a sharp sigh. "How's that for helpful?"

"The road will be washed out from the rain, so getting footprints or tire tracks won't happen, either." He took a sip of coffee.

"Which means whoever was there remains anonymous until they strike again."

"We'll get the sheriff involved," he said. "That'll get more eyes on the case."

It wasn't exactly progress, but she couldn't be picky under the circumstances. She was still beating herself up for not checking the weather before leaving the house. What kind of parent would she make? Not that she wanted children at this point in her life, or possibly ever. Ruling them out didn't feel like the right move.

She glanced over at Rue, who seemed the most content in Kit's arms.

"She's a good baby," Kit said, practically beaming. "All she needed was a meal and a diaper change to be happy."

"I think you're selling yourself short, Kit. She's comfortable with you. She was screaming the whole time I held her." Not technically the whole time, but it sure felt like it.

Kit issued a grunt. "She's probably worn out from crying, then."

"Do you want to sit down?" Blaize asked.

"Yes." She had questions for the gorgeous man. But something told her that he wouldn't have the answers she needed to hear to be able to walk away from Rue.

Chapter Four

"Do you want a refill?" Blaize nodded toward Carys's empty mug.

"Yes, please." She smiled, and it lit up her face, stirring something in his chest. An attraction wasn't just inconvenient; it was out of the question.

He fixed her a cup and joined them at the table, sitting across from her.

"Thank you," she said before taking a sip. The little mewl that passed over those pink heart-shaped lips stirred him in other places.

Great job, Wilde! Way to keep it in check.

"You are convinced that you're not the father," Carys started after a furtive glance toward Kit.

"I'm absolutely sure." No question.

"May I ask how?"

"How old is she?" he asked.

"Three months."

"And how long does it take for one of those things to cook?"

Carys's eyebrow shot up. "Forty weeks if the pregnancy goes to full term." Her finger absently traced around the rim of the mug as she studied him, head tilted to one side.

He performed a mental calculation. "So, basically, a week more than nine months."

"That sounds right," she said. "I don't have personal experience to draw from, but it checks out with my mental math."

"For me to be the father, I would have had to have sex with the mother almost exactly this day last year."

Kit coughed at the outright mention of sex.

He glanced her way. "Forgive me for being direct."

Her cheeks flushed and she giggled. "I've heard worse. You just caught me off guard."

Turning his attention back toward Carys, whose crimson cheeks were sexy as hell, he said, "I'm certain that I didn't father a child because that would require having sex with a stranger not long after I buried my wife. I got to know one person during that time, but believe me when I say nothing came of it."

Carys brought her hand up to cover a gasp. "I'm so sorry. I had no idea."

"Now you know." He didn't normally shout his business from the rooftop. Blaize wasn't exactly the sharing type.

Kit's girlish smile wiped from her face. "I thought she left you."

He shook his head. Now his private business was out there for anyone to see. Great.

"Why didn't you tell me?" Kit asked.

"Lynn had been sick for a while." He shrugged. "It was something we were going through."

His wife had been fiery, opinionated, and almost wholly unpredictable. The first time he'd drummed up the courage to call her after a week of texting, the phone shook in his hands.

Lynn had been beautiful and carefree. She'd been the

opposite of the women he'd gone for in the past. His exes were country down to their souls. Lynn was adventure and excitement. Falling for her hadn't taken but a minute.

As they got to know each other, he uncovered a different side to her—serious and more calculated. A side that thought about every move intensely before making it. The dual sides of her personality had thrown him for a loop at first. But he'd already fallen for her and figured he would never be bored loving someone like her.

The truth had been a little more brutal when the first diagnosis came. Bipolar disorder wasn't something he was familiar with, but Lynn's highs and lows along with her risk-taking behavior made more sense to him once he educated himself on the disorder. Lynn was charismatic like no one he'd ever known on the highs, and she hit rock bottom on the lows.

Blaize and her doctor had gotten his wife on a good regimen with her meds. Life began to resemble something that looked a lot like normal. He'd let himself wonder if the two of them could think about starting a family together. Until the worst diagnosis came the next year. The one that was rarely survivable. The one there was no good medication for. The one that hit hard and fast. They'd tried everything they could think of to slow the illness down and wipe it out. Looking back, he'd tried. Lynn had gone along with whatever he said. The experimental drug didn't work, nor did the clinical trial. Traditional Chinese medicine had no good answers. Acupuncture was a bust as well as half a dozen other far-fetched therapies. No amount of yoga, hypnotherapy, or Reiki could fix her.

They ran out of options. But Lynn had given up almost the day she'd learned about her illness. Part of him still resented her for it.

He looked up and realized he had two pairs of eyes trained on him, waiting for his response. "What good would it have done to bring anyone else down?"

"You wouldn't have had to go through it alone," Kit said in practically a whisper with the kind of reverence normally reserved for talking during church service.

"I knew you were there if I needed you." Those words rang hollow. He had wallowed in self-pity for too many months after Lynn's death. He'd cursed everyone and everything that had once been sacred to him.

"That's not the same thing, and you know it." Kit's scolding tone struck a chord.

"You're right," he said. "I should have told you everything."

"I knew Lynn was sick and that you'd had your ups and downs, but I didn't know it was…" Her voice trailed up as she looked at him with the sincerest eyes. "Explains a lot about the last couple of years."

He nodded. He knew she was talking about the way he'd withdrawn from her and everyone else. The lack of communication with his family. The way he'd treated brothers who didn't take his calls now.

A dawn of understanding passed behind Kit's eyes.

Rather than keep going down a path that couldn't be undone, he shifted the conversation to the real reason Carys was here. "I'm confident that I wasn't sleeping around a year ago. And now you know the reason. But that leaves this little girl in limbo, doesn't it?"

"Officially? Yes."

"What about unofficially?"

"You haven't taken a paternity test to prove you're not the biological father so I have no reason to disregard your name on the birth certificate." She put a hand up to stop him from protesting. “I’m not saying you are. I believe you’re being honest. However, I have a government document that implicates you as the father and no DNA test to disprove it.” She looked at him with pleading eyes. “If you are officially not the father, then Rue goes to a seriously understaffed orphanage while I hunt down next of kin. You are a good person. You came to the aid of a stranger in this horrific storm. Not many people would risk their own safety under these circumstances. In fact, most wouldn’t have called back.”

“The name Stephanie Cross suddenly rings a bell,” he said, catching on and appreciating the show of confidence in him. If he could buy some time for Carys to find a suitable home for Rue, he wouldn’t stand in the way. It felt like he could finally do something good for someone else. He felt useful for the first time in a long time.

Carys shot him a look. “What are you saying?”

“I was hitting a lot of bars a year ago. Drinking more than my fair share.” His admission got a stern look from Kit. “I’m not proud of it, but I figure honesty is the best policy.”

“And this is true?” Carys asked.

He raised his right hand with three middle fingers extended while his thumb held down his pinky finger in the Scout Sign. “Hand to god.”

“Okay, I can work with that narrative,” she said on a slow exhale, needing to revise her report.

Blaize caught Kit’s gaze. “You okay with a baby staying here for…what?” He looked to Carys.

“A couple of days, maybe more,” she said. “Next of kin will have to be found, then notified of Stephanie’s death if that proves to be the case, and I can screen them for suitability. This girl is too young to remember anything that we do for her, but believe me when I say it'll matter in the long run more than you can know."

The heaviness in those words struck Blaize. Had Carys lost someone important to her at a young age?

"It'll be nice to have a little one around again," Kit said. "We haven't had a crib in this house in a lot of years. Your father got rid of everything I kept for you and your brothers. Said this wasn't a storage facility."

Carys noted the tick in Blaize's jaw at the mention of his father. She would mention that safety standards were different now and it wasn't advised to use cribs and such that were decades old if that would make it better. Based on his tense expression, it wouldn't. This conversation was bigger and had more weight. It was about casually throwing away memories. She got it. Her father hadn't been any better. He'd gotten rid of all Carys's memorabilia, too.

"You'll have to tell me when you're ready to take the DNA test," she said to Blaize. "I appreciate you buying time for me."

Thunder cracked.

"Do you want to settle in for the night?" Kit asked, surprising Carys with the question.

"I don't have any clothes or supplies for myself," she stammered. "I'm sure the storm will blow over, and then maybe…"

When she really thought about it, she needed to stay. Kit would be fine taking care of Rue. Still, leaving felt strangely like abandonment. Was it because paternity hadn't been established? Was that the niggling feeling in the back of Carys's mind warning her to stick close to Rue? Did it have to do with guilt for pushing an infant on a family where she didn't technically belong?

Definitely all of those things. She couldn't imagine walking out that door, going home, and getting any sleep tonight. Especially not after what happened. Was her car even drivable?

"On second thought, I'd love to take you up on your generosity," she said. "Thank you for your hospitality."

Kit smiled as her gaze bounced from Carys to Blaize and back. "It sure is nice to have a few more females in the house for a change." She seemed to catch the implication of her casual comment when she shook her head. She flashed her eyes at Blaize. "I don't think that came out right."

"No offense taken," he said warmly. He clearly cared a great deal about his grandmother. He'd lost a wife. It hadn't dawned on Carys to ask if he had any other children.

Kit motioned for help with the baby. Blaize was by her side, helping her place Rue in the carrier. For a man of his size, he was surprisingly gentle with his grandmother and the baby.

For a split second, Carys was sure she saw something in his eyes that looked a lot like longing when he looked down at Rue. Had to be a mistake on her part.

When Kit left the room, Carys figured it was a good time to ask the questions on her mind. She remembered how much her father drank on certain days that she would later realize was her mother's birthday and their wedding anniversary. Forget major holidays. Those were never the same.

"I wouldn't be doing my job properly if I didn't ask a couple of questions," she said, wincing. They'd extended hospitality to her and Rue. The last thing she wanted to do was slap them in the face with rude questions.

"Okay-y-y."

"It's just…the thing is…"

Wow, she was really winning with words, wasn't she?

"Were you serious about going out drinking this time last year?"

"Yes," he said. It dawned on him where she was going with this. "I can admit that I drank too much when I was swimming in loss and self-pity."

"Where did you hang out?"

"Austin bars mostly," he said.

"Do you mind making a list?"

"What good would that do?" His right eyebrow hiked up.

"I need to track down information about Stephanie and—"

"You think it's possible I was so drunk that I don't remember having sex with her." The disappointment in his voice stabbed her.

"It's nothing personal," she said, hearing the defensiveness in her own voice. "If she listed you on the birth certificate, you must have had some contact with her."

He exhaled a slow breath. His eyebrows pinched together as he pursed thick, kissable lips. "That's a reasonable guess."

Carys cleared the sudden dryness in her throat. "I'm at a loss as to figuring out who her relatives are. I'll take any thread I can get no matter how loose it might be."

"What are you saying?" he asked. "Stephanie Cross might be a cover?"

"It could be that or someone who wanted to disappear," she said. "It's not impossible to create an identity. Forgers are amazing with identification nowadays."

"Is that what you really think?"

"I have no list of next of kin and a name on a birth certificate for a father who swears he's never heard of this person," she said. "I don't know what to think but Rue deserves for me to do everything I can to make sure her mother isn't alive somewhere, hiding."

"What do you make of the person you said was trying to get inside your vehicle?" he asked.

Carys was just now letting herself begin to think about the possibilities there. "Could have been someone stranded in the storm and panicking."

He nodded. Then he stared out the window. "It's possible. I didn't see a vehicle anywhere near."

"I don't remember passing a stranded car, either."

"Someone is out there and could be watching the house," he said.

Creepy crawlies ran wild up and down her spine at the thought.

"It's time to make that call to the sheriff," he said.

Did that mean she wasn't safe here?

Chapter Five

Blaize listened intently as Carys recounted the story of what happened on her way to the ranch on the phone with the sheriff. This place's bad luck seemed to be rubbing off on everyone who came near. It also occurred to him that he should try calling his brothers again. They needed to be part of the decision-making process when it came to all things dealing with the ranch, which would be happening soon if they were going to keep this place up and running.

He highly doubted Raiden or Phoenix would care about their father's death. Not one of the man's sons could stand to be in the same room with him. Cormac was a piece of work. From the initial look of things, he would create about as much havoc in death as he did in life.

Inheritances were tricky, especially when you were handed something broken. The one thing that was worth saving on this place was Kit. She deserved the world. More of that familiar guilt zinged him at the thought of how badly he'd shut everyone out of his life. Updates on social media weren't his thing, either. He didn't live his life for "likes" or any other type of approval. Hell, he barely used his phone's camera.

One thing was certain—he needed to quit licking his wounds over losing Lynn. He needed to figure out how to put that chapter of his life behind him. Because he'd blacked out a couple of times after a drinking binge last year. Always woke up fully dressed but not always in his own apartment. A park bench? Yes. The back seat of his Jeep? Affirmative.

Was he proud of this?

No.

He tuned into Carys as she concluded her statement to the sheriff. The call ended with Carys promising to call or text with any updates of if the mystery person appeared again. Blaize had paid close attention to the names she'd given the sheriff. Three men.

"What was that about?" he asked.

"What?"

"The names?" He probably shouldn't press the issue, but she'd gotten up close and personal with his business. Turnabout seemed like fair play.

"The sheriff asked about the last person I dated and anyone who asked me out but was refused, with a special note toward anyone who persisted."

"Sounds like he believes this could be personal," Blaize said.

She nodded. "Apparently most crimes against women are committed by someone they know and trust."

The thought of a man hurting the person he was supposed to care about burned him from the inside out. "Makes me sick to think about what happens to women at the hands of men."

"Agreed," she said, a little of the fight gone from her voice. It was replaced with something that sounded a lot like sorrow.

His hands fisted at the thought of someone harming her.

"And what do you think?" he asked, forcing a calm he

didn't feel. "Could this mystery person be someone you know?" A stalker?

Carys issued a sharp sigh. "Anything's possible, I guess." She hugged her arms to her chest. "I'd hate to think someone I know would follow me…track my moves." She shivered. "That's awful."

Unfortunately, it wasn't just possible, it was likely. He made a mental note of the names she'd mentioned to the sheriff: James Gray. Ethan York. Gabe Hutchins. Blaize would do a little digging on the internet later. See what he could find out about these men.

"It's a reality that shouldn't exist," he said. "Women should be able to leave their doors unlocked and not have to worry. They sure as hell shouldn't have to live their lives in fear of the opposite sex." Too many times, they did. And it angered him beyond belief.

He glanced at the clock, realized it was dinner time. "Are you hungry?"

"I should probably try to eat something," she said. "Wish I'd been more prepared. I hate to be a burden."

"You couldn't be." He waved a hand, dismissing the idea. Since going out to the grocery wasn't an option, he checked the fridge to see what he could pull together. "We might have to get creative since I got in late last night and haven't had a chance to go to the store."

She blinked at him. "You don't normally live here?"

"I do now," he said before shaking his head. "It's complicated."

"I'm sure I can understand."

"My father passed away and left this place to his three sons." That was it in a nutshell.

"I'm sorry."

"About my father? Don't be."

Again she blinked, looking unsure what to say or where to begin. And then she said, "I totally understand complicated family dynamics. You don't have to explain further if you don't want to, but I'm here if you want someone to listen."

He thought about it for a second, decided it might be a welcome change of topic from the stresses of the day for her. But first, "How do you like breakfast for dinner?"

"Is that a serious question?" She laughed. The sound was almost musical.

"I guess not."

He started pulling out what little supplies were there. Knowing this was all the food in the house brought on more of that guilt that he'd been so focused on his own sorrow that he hadn't been making sure Kit was okay. He would never forgive himself if she went to bed hungry because he was too wrapped up in his own life to notice. Cormac sure as hell couldn't take care of anyone else.

Blaize should have known better. He should have stopped by to make sure Kit had everything she needed.

It didn't take long to whip up the omelets. He toasted bagels that looked dangerously close to being too old. He set out an almost-empty jar of jelly. There were a few hot dogs left that subbed for sausage. He cut them up and served them alongside breakfast. Lastly, he had one can of pork and beans.

"This is a feast," Carys said. "What can I do to help?"

"Set out the plates and then fill yours." He motioned toward the cabinet, thinking how nice it was to have someone who was eager to do their part. From day one, he'd taken care of Lynn. He'd overheard her bragging to a friend that she didn't have to lift a finger around the house. Looking back, she'd allowed him to step in and do everything since for her. He never knew which version of her would show up in a given hour. He'd loved her and made a commitment when he said his vows. So, no regrets.

"Thank you for pitching in, by the way," he said to Carys.

"I literally did nothing." She shook her head, but the way the corners of her mouth upturned made him grin.

Kit waltzed in. "Something smells good in here."

"I was just about to call for you," he said as he cut off the stovetop. "You have perfect timing." He motioned toward the table. "Take a seat."

Kit smiled before doing as asked. "Guess I get the princess treatment today."

Carys put down placemats and set the table, put on a fresh pot of coffee, and joined them. "This does smell amazing."

Those words caused his chest to puff up with pride. He glanced around the table and couldn't help thinking this was what he'd had in mind years ago when he thought about having a family.

Whoa! Talk about putting the cart before the horse.

This seemed like a good time to remind himself this wasn't his family with the exception of Kit. The kid wasn't his, and Carys was just doing her job.

If that had to become a mantra, so be it.

It was a shame Blaize might not be Rue's father. Sitting here at the table with him and Kit gave Carys all the warm-and-fuzzy feelings she hoped for when she walked into a place where she had to make an assessment and leave a child.

The need for repairs made more sense now that she knew Blaize drove in last night after learning his father had recently passed. The house had a homey quality despite the disrepair. Places had a feeling, and it had everything to do with the people occupying the space. In two years on the job, she'd walked into filth. This place was tidy.

One glance at the way Blaize looked at his grandmother told Carys everything she needed to know about how much he respected her. And she adored her grandson right back. Even without her mother in the picture, this would have been an amazing place for Rue to grow up.

Carys believed Blaize would get this home in tip-top shape. All it needed was a hammer, some nails, and a little elbow grease—sweat equity.

"Thanks for cooking, Blaize." Kit stood up. She must've moved a little too fast because she swayed. Before she could fall, Carys was at her side with a firm hand on the older woman's back.

"Are you okay?" The concern in Blaize's voice melted a little more of the ice encasing Carys's heart.

"I'm fine." Kit tried to play it off like it was nothing. "Here, let me help with dishes."

"Sorry, no can do," Carys said. "I'm on dish duty. Gotta earn my keep if I'm going to stay the night."

"Don't be silly. You're a guest." Kit grabbed onto Carys's hand as she took a step back from the table.

"It would make me feel better about imposing if you let me take this one." Carys helped Kit across the room. "Plus, it's way too early to end your princess treatment. How often does this come around?"

Kit smiled. "My head would swell so big we'd have to cut holes in the doors if I was treated like this every day."

"Exactly, so you might as well enjoy it while it lasts." Carys returned the smile, hiding her concern for the older woman. "Tell me where we're headed, and it would be my honor to escort you, Your Highness."

"Into the living room, if you don't mind," Kit said, mustering a voice that was surely meant to sound royal.

Carys made a production out of helping her into the next room and into a worn leather recliner. A TV tray with remote and a book sat next to the chair. "Can I get you anything before I take my leave, Highness?"

"This'll do for now, but thank you." Kit winked and then picked up the remote. "I'm hooked on a crime series."

"I'll leave you to your binge-watching." Carys gave a little curtsy before leaving the room and rejoining a concerned-looking Blaize.

His face was ghost white as he stood with his backside against the bullnose counter. He white-knuckled the edge.

Carys studied him for a moment before speaking. "I got your grandmother settled."

Sounds from the TV drifted in from the next room.

"I appreciate it," he said in barely more than a whisper. The tension in his tone said he was stressed to the gills and ready to snap. "She didn't say anything about being sick."

"It's possible she just stood up too fast, don't you think?"

A muscle ticked in his jaw. His gaze dropped to the ground. Tension radiated off him in palpable waves.

"I don't know, and I highly doubt she'll tell me now that she knows about Lynn." He barely ground out the words.

"Why would you think that?" Carys asked, keeping her tone as calm and neutral as possible.

"She would believe she is only adding to my stress," he said.

"Those are very different situations," she said.

Shaking his head, he said, "She won't see it that way." He compressed his lips, forming a severe line. "My gut tells me that she is hiding a serious medical condition."

Could be fear or a form of PTSD after losing his wife

to illness. As much as she wanted to offer some type of comforting words, she didn't want to give false hope. Kit might've been sick. Or her age might've been catching up to her. Or she might've just been tired. All three were plausible reasons for her moments of weakness.

The storm had created a lot of excitement.

"Is Kit your grandmother on your father's side?" she asked.

"Yes, but I don't see how that..."

He stopped midsentence as though a few dots were connecting that her loss coupled with the stress of all the changes coming could have thrown her off balance.

"She might not be sleeping well," Carys said. "I know when I'm tired, I wobble. Actually, it's very much like me to walk into walls in the morning before I get my first cup of coffee down."

Losing his grandmother after losing a wife and a father would be too much for anyone. Blaize might not have been close to his father or care one way or another whether the man lived or died, but unresolved relationships were almost worse. She couldn't imagine losing the person you were meant to spend the rest of your life with, especially while still so young.

Carys closed the distance between them in a couple of quick strides. Witnessing the pain in his eyes up close was going to be a mistake. It caused her to reach for his hand. He tugged her toward him, keeping his gaze locked onto hers.

Were they two broken souls who recognized each other from a place somewhere deep?

"I'm sorry for everything you've been through, Blaize."

He gave a slight nod.

"And I would very much like to ask for a kiss right now."

"What's stopping you?" he asked.

"Fear that you'll say no."

He took in a slow breath. "You don't ever have to be afraid of me." His voice was low, gravelly, sexy.

Kissing him would be unprofessional if he turned out to be Rue's father.

"Is it okay if I do this?" he asked, bringing his hands up to frame her face. His eyes glistened with something that looked a whole lot like need.

"Yes."

His tongue slicked across his bottom lip. The man was sexy as hell.

"About that kiss," he said.

"What about it?"

"I'm going to need your clear permission first."

"Yes. Definitely yes. One hundred percent yes," she said.

It was all the encouragement he needed. A small smile toyed with the corners of his lips—those perfect lips. The top of which formed a perfect Cupid's bow.

In the next second, his mouth pressed so tenderly against hers it robbed her breath and dissolved the last bit of resolve she had left.

Chapter Six

Blaize grazed his teeth across Carys's bottom lip. The little mewl that escaped her mouth was tinder to fire. He teased his tongue inside her mouth. She tasted like dark roast coffee and honey, his new favorite flavor.

He dropped his hands, splaying them across her back instead. She arched, pressing full breasts against his chest. Pulling back enough to catch his breath, he leaned his forehead against hers.

Her hands came up to his shoulders, fingernails digging in as though she needed to anchor herself.

"Kissing you is the best thing that's happened to me in too long" came out in a rasp as he tried, and failed, to catch his breath. Need welled up like a rogue spring storm, threatening to devastate everything in its wake.

The moment of pause brought on a wave of guilt. He bit back a curse. A child's future hung in the balance, and he could scarcely keep his hands off her caretaker. Did that make him a jerk? Or did it make him human?

"What is it? What's wrong?" Carys asked, as if sensing the mental debate going on in his head.

"It sure as hell isn't you," he said, hoping that gave her enough clarification to drop the subject without hurt feelings.

She took a step back; a sudden chill sat between them.

She folded her arms and challenged him with her glare. "Don't bother with the 'it's me and not you' speech. That would hurt my feelings."

Blaize let out a sharp sigh. "Can I make a confession?"

"Please do." She shifted in posture like she was steeling herself to absorb a punch.

Dammit. He hadn't meant for something this mind-blowing to turn into an insult.

"You're the best thing that's happened to me in a very long time, and I don't want to do anything to screw that up." His honesty caught him off guard. "That…and my choices in love haven't exactly paid dividends." Should he tell her the feelings he had for her were as foreign as a poetry slam? That he'd loved his wife but never felt this mix of excitement and ease when they'd first started dating?

"You're a dangerous man, Blaize."

That was all she said before she turned around and walked off. He heard her voice in the next room as she talked with Kit. And then all he could hear was the TV.

Blaize walked over to the sleeping baby in the carrier. She was an angel with just a hint of dark hair. This little girl deserved a loving home. She deserved the world but was an orphan for the time being.

It nearly broke his heart when she took in a breath. Her face crunched like she was about to wind up to cry again like a pitcher at the plate, but then she settled. Her eyes remained closed. There'd been so much excitement, he'd forgotten to ask for a picture of Stephanie Cross. If the woman named him on her daughter's birth certificate, it stood to reason he knew her. The name drew a blank. Cross could be her married name. Did he know any Stephanies?

He had to reach all the way back to high school to pull out a name: Stephanie Ambler. Seemed like everyone had a social media page these days. Could he find her? He picked up his cell and pulled up the most popular one, figuring he'd start there.

Stephanie Ambler, now Smith, posted pictures regularly on her account. A quick flip before the app told him he needed to log in to continue revealed she had three children. The oldest one had a pimply face and looked to be in his early teens. Two daughters, twins, who looked to be a couple years younger than their brother rounded out the family.

While there, he looked up the names he'd overheard Carys provide to the sheriff. No James Gray in the immediate area that he could find. Since Blaize didn't do social media, he couldn't exactly label anyone else who didn't a serial killer. The only app he'd used was for dating. It had been the way he met his wife.

Next he checked Ethan Hutchins. A few names came up, none in this area. Same for Gabe York.

He closed the app.

Glancing over at the spot where he and Carys had shared a kiss so laced with promise and pleasure brought back the memory of it—a memory that set the bar for all future kisses.

Guilt stabbed him. The same pang he felt every time he laughed or thought about moving on with life after Lynn's death. Getting a handle on the ranch might be just the win he needed. He could use a new lease on life.

Blaize started out of the room, made it halfway across before he froze. Was he allowed to leave the baby alone in a room?

Taking her into the living room might wake her up. She was sleeping so peacefully. He didn't want to do anything to disturb her peace. He also needed a shower and at least a few hours of sleep. Watching over Lynn, he'd gotten used to running on five hours if he could close his eyes for twenty minutes here and there.

Since he wasn't sure he could leave the baby and he didn't want to call for Kit, he sat down at the table. Head in hands, he shut his eyes. The image of the kiss was burned into the backs of his lids.

More of that inconvenient need welled up.

Carys was intelligent and caring. Her beauty was beyond anything he'd witnessed before, inside and out. She had a way of looking at him that stripped him bare.

On a practical level, she was probably a decade younger and just getting started in her career. Having a family most likely wasn't on her radar. He'd stopped considering having one when Lynn became sick. At thirty-five, he figured the window was closing since he didn't see himself marrying again. It was all too hard. The vow *for better or worse* meant the world to him. When he gave his word, he didn't take it back.

Even if a relationship could happen between him and Carys—and that was a big *if*—they were in different places in life.

Damn, Wilde. You really went down a rabbit hole. Time to suck it up and get realistic. A kiss like the one they shared needed to be a one-off event. Period. Plus, she was already breaking too many rules as it was. He didn't need to add to it or cost her job. He'd overstepped with the kiss. No matter how much he wanted it to happen again, it couldn't.

EMBARRASSMENT STILL HEATED Carys's cheeks despite the long shower. Kit had laid out clean clothes in the guest bedroom, which were lifesavers. Never underestimate the power of light joggers and an oversized T-shirt when it came to comfort clothes. They were basically a cotton hug.

The kiss she shared—*No! Asked for*—still burned on her lips in the best possible way, like he'd marked her as his. The rejection afterward stung worse than falling onto a fire ant mound.

Carys needed to pluck up the courage to go back into the kitchen and check on Rue. She listened in case the baby needed her. Everything was quiet. Peaceful. Except for the chirps of crickets and other insects outside the window. The noise used to freak her out when she'd first moved out of the city. Now? They were like a lullaby.

Going into the kitchen might mean facing Blaize again. So soon?

Carys had learned over the years to rip off the Band-Aid when faced with something that might be uncomfortable. Why was that suddenly a problem now?

Blaize. The man stirred foreign feelings—feelings that had her asking to kiss the father of her ward. How was that for professionalism? The worst part was that she couldn't stop thinking about what it felt like when their mouths fused together. She'd never believed a relationship could complete her. She was already a fully formed human who didn't need another half to feel whole. This thing between her and Blaize was something else, something deeper.

Giving herself a mental headshake to clear those thoughts, she headed toward the kitchen.

Kit had fallen asleep in front of the TV. Carys grabbed the blanket off the back of the couch and placed it on top of Kit, who instantly relaxed. The AC window unit in the living room was still on, in addition to a ceiling fan. Kit would end up sick at this rate.

Considering the lack of noise, she wondered if Blaize had gone to bed. Would he leave the kitchen light on? The baby unattended?

Rounding the corner, she stopped mid-step as her gaze landed on the image in front of her. Blaize had his arm extended over the table, his head resting on it, using it as a pillow. His eyes were closed, and his even breathing said he was asleep.

Rue was still in the carrier that he'd placed on the floor and scooted next to him. It was a shame Blaize didn't believe he was the girl's father. Between this scene and the longing she'd seen in his eyes earlier when he'd looked at the baby, he was more than ready to be a father.

Instead, he'd lost a wife. Life played some seriously cruel jokes sometimes. She'd walked into plenty of houses with kids where the father figure was so checked out he could barely be forced to step away from the TV screen to meet with her. She was a basketball fan. She understood team loyalty. She also knew how easy it was to record a game and save it for later.

Having walked into dozens of families' lives in her two years on the job, she'd seen the highest and the lowest forms of parenting. The worst of them neglected their children and provided filthy homes with just enough food to get by. The best of them provided loving, caring environments that allowed the children to find their passions and know they always had support.

What was that like?

Her father had become a tyrant and a warden. On some basic level, Carys realized he'd become overprotective after losing the love of his life. He'd overcorrected and become detached. Based on the few pictures she'd seen from before she was born, it was hard to believe he was the same person. Pain had an interesting effect on people. In her father's case, it hardened him. His fear came out as anger. She knew that now.

Still, it was difficult to forgive him for all the damage he caused. It didn't help matters that he hadn't tried to reach out or make their relationship right. Once she walked out the door, he stuck to his threat of disowning her and cutting her off.

Families were complicated. And yet she couldn't help but wonder how different her life might have been had her mother been alive. Would she have made a difference in the manner in which Carys had been brought up?

Would there have been laughter in the house? Holidays with large Christmas trees that they would have decorated together? Hot chocolate by a fireplace?

Would her father smile more? Or at all?

Would she know what it was like to have someone fight for her in parent-teacher meetings rather than ice her out on the way home if she got one bad report?

A crash outside caused her to gasp. Blaize's head popped up. He wiped his eyes.

"What happened?" he asked.

She flipped off the kitchen light, crouched low, and nodded toward the back door. "Someone's out there."

Blaize was on his feet and making a beeline for the back door in two seconds flat. He grabbed a butcher knife out of the block on the countertop before exiting.

Carys was torn between going to the baby or following Blaize. Based on his size and physical strength, he could handle himself in pretty much any situation. What if he brought a knife to a gun fight?

That would be a problem she couldn't solve with her presence.

What if he was surprised? Caught off guard? In a physical fight with someone much larger than he was?

What if someone slipped inside and stole the baby?

Rue was in Carys's charge. She crawled to the baby and sat next to the carrier. It dawned on her that she might need a weapon.

Panic gripped her as she popped up long enough to get a knife. It occurred to her that she should have checked to see if the front door was locked. The sheriff's questions nailed her. *Have you interacted with anyone lately who might want to do you harm? Have you been in a disagreement with anyone? Have you rejected anyone?*

Three names had come to mind. The first was a father who'd lost custody of his child based on her recommendation. Veiled threats in this job were becoming surprisingly commonplace. Gabe Hutchins hadn't threatened her with words. There was no evidence or no way to prove he was out for her. It was more in the way he'd stood there, arms crossed, pure evil in his eyes. The slight sneer. The way he picked her apart with his gaze.

Feeling threatened by someone's presence wasn't the same as being threatened. She'd confided in Harrison, and he'd basically patted her on top of the head and told her not to let her imagination get the best of her.

The next person, James Gray, was someone she'd dated who couldn't seem to let go. They'd gone out a few times after both had swiped on each other's dating profile. The whole situation had been casual for her until she realized he was building a narrative about them being in a relationship. A handful of dates didn't equate to being a couple. James confused the situation despite her being upfront about not being open to anything serious at the time. She was interested in casual dating, good dinner conversation, and that was about it. With the right person, she'd consider adding sex to the equation. She wasn't in a hurry for a relationship while she was busy building a career. Swiping on James's profile turned out to be a huge mistake. It had been quiet lately, though. She thought he'd gotten the hint.

And then there was Ethan York. He came to mind almost immediately when the sheriff asked if there was anyone she felt threatened by. One of her first cases, she'd helped him get into a halfway house as he timed out of the system. She'd graduated college at twenty-two years old. Ethan had just turned eighteen. He had obsessive-compulsive tendencies and had developed the belief that the two of them were destined to be together. He'd mistaken her sympathy for his situation for a love connection. He was impulsive and had poor emotional regulation, coupled with low self-esteem. If she could go back, there was so much she would do differently this time. She'd been green, a newbie, and it had cost her.

Last Carys heard, he was in jail after being caught with drugs. Maybe it was time to check his status, see if he got released.

Any of those three could fit the vague description of the person wearing the hoodie earlier.

She listened for any signs of a fight outside as more panic gripped her. It was quiet. Too quiet. What the hell was happening out there?

Should she turn around and alert Kit to the potential danger?

The baby stirred.

No. No. No. This is not a good time to draw attention to the kitchen.

Moving her might wake her up. At this point, there was a chance she would stay asleep.

One look at the baby said otherwise. Rue's face twisted, scrunched, before she sucked in a deep breath and then belted out an ear-splitting cry.

Chapter Seven

Blaize slipped around the perimeter of the house, searching for any signs of life. Crickets chirped along with the usual sounds of night in the country. He didn't see any movement other than trees bending to the heavy wind gusts. Stacks of old paint cans next to the back door had been scattered like bowling pins. He couldn't remember if it had been like that earlier but suspected it wasn't.

Heavy rain meant wet soil, making footprints next to impossible to stick. Besides, he would have walked all over them by now anyway. The mud would mold them together.

And that was *if* someone was out here. His thoughts snapped to the hoodie-wearing individual from earlier. This person made the most sense. And then he considered the names Carys had given the sheriff as possible suspects.

He made a mental note to ask more about them in the morning.

Everyone needed to get a good night of sleep so they could wake up early and get cracking. If the threat had moved closer to the house, he intended to figure out who the hell was behind it and stop them before someone got hurt. He would never forgive himself if harm came to Kit. Carys might've been a firecracker on the outside, but her devotion to protecting a child she didn't know more than twenty-four hours ago said she had a soft side that the hard shell was no doubt meant to protect.

Sounds of the baby crying penetrated through the back door as he opened it. He resisted the urge to run toward her. Instead, he glanced around the room, surprised when he didn't see Carys next to the child. His eyes had adjusted to the dark, making it easy to see clearly.

It dawned on him that someone could be inside the house. They could be holding Carys hostage. She wouldn't leave the baby alone, crying without good reason.

Taking a step inside, the floorboard creaked underneath his weight.

From the corner of his eye, he saw a figure leaping at him from around the bottom cabinet. The glint of metal caught his eye. A knife.

Survival instinct took over. He brought his forearm up to block his face.

Carys's face came into view, a panicked look in her eyes. It was as though her brain and hand disconnected. Her face read *Stop.* Her arm kept going.

Blaize ducked in time to miss the swipe. He sidestepped her, grabbing her wrist after her hand passed above his hair.

"Are you trying to give me a haircut?" He managed to growl the words at her. On some level, he realized that she was in full-on defensive mode. He'd seen how protective she'd been with the baby first and then his grandmother. Still. She'd known he was outside and would then presumably come back in. She should've been more careful because he had no intention of ending up in the hospital. "Or brain surgery?"

"I'm sorry," she said through a gasp. "I didn't know it was you, and I wasn't sure if anything happened. And then Rue started crying." Her gaze darted from him to the baby. She held up a hand before rushing over to console the little thing.

For something so tiny, she sure had a great pair of lungs.

She plugged the kid up with some type of rubber contraption. He's seen them before but had no idea what they were called. This was one of many reasons he probably shouldn't be a father.

When his wife became sick, the possibility had been stripped from him. He'd made his peace with it, figuring he would never love again. A family was a lot of work. To his mind, he knew he couldn't keep a kid alive for the first few years without a partner to do it with. He had a ton of respect for anyone doing it alone. Single parents were rock stars in his book.

"There," Carys said with a satisfied smile, bringing his thoughts back to the present. She bit back a yawn.

"You should get some sleep," he said, hearing the grumpy tone in his own voice. Damn if she didn't rattle him in ways he wasn't ready to face. Better to snap at her than kiss her again because the temptation was a real threat. From now on, he'd maintain a safe distance. Physically. Emotionally. Mentally.

"You, too," Carys said softly, still staring at the baby. "She's an angel."

His gaze stayed trained on Carys. "I couldn't agree more."

He thought about telling her about looking for a picture of Stephanie Cross on social media to jog a memory and decided the update could wait until morning. "How often does one of those things wake up in the middle of the night?"

Carys exhaled a slow breath. "I have no idea. I guess we'll figure it out together."

He liked the sound of those words a little too much for his own good. "Will you take her to bed with you?"

"I think that's best for tonight."

Kit yelled out in her sleep from the living room. Blaize made a beeline for his grandmother. He checked her over as her eyelids fluttered, couldn't find anything immediately concerning. A bad dream?

He should get her to her own room where she'd be more comfortable. As he scooped her up, he realized she'd had an accident. The back of her pants was wet.

He'd seen worse. Cleaned up worse.

Kit's eyes fluttered open. Her face soured. "Cormac. What's going on with you? Who is here with you?"

"It's your grandson Blaize. Remember?" There was no way he wanted her thinking her son was here. Cormac couldn't keep a cactus alive in the sun.

"What?" Kit tried to focus her eyes but appeared to be struggling. "What are you doing here?"

He carried her to a secondary bedroom. Cormac had moved her once he took over the ranch, and it was one of many reasons Blaize and his brothers didn't visit. They didn't like setting foot in Cormac's home. When Blaize stopped by before Lynn got sick, he would stay outside for the duration of the visit. If he did step in the house, it was to go to the bathroom or grab a cup of coffee in the kitchen.

The thought of his grandmother being kicked out of her own bedroom made him angry to this day. *Your mother deserved better from you, asshole.*

If Blaize's mother had been interested in more than a drinking buddy, he would have done anything for the woman. By age seventeen, he'd lost track of her. She'd gotten into harder substances and didn't exactly keep up a social media page or a steady phone number for that matter. She had, however, tracked him down on his nineteenth birthday to ask for a loan. Made some excuse about not getting paid for another week and needing food.

Fool that he'd been at that age, he had believed she remembered his birthday and called for that reason. Nope. She wanted money. Wanted him to send it via an app. He ended the call telling her not to reach out again. She hadn't.

He cut across the hallway to the adjacent bathroom. The air was still moist from the shower Carys had taken earlier, and the scent of lavender shampoo filled his senses. He balanced on one leg and managed to close the commode lid before setting Kit down.

"Go on. I can manage from here," she instructed. Was she embarrassed to get undressed in front of him? Of course she was. Kit was prideful.

How could he manage to help her and salvage her pride—pride that had no doubt taken a hit when she lost her bladder. It wasn't a big deal to him, but he understood.

"What can I grab for you from the bedroom?" he asked, realizing she would dig her heels in.

"My gowns are in the top drawer and my undergarments are in the smaller one right below it." She sat with her back straight despite being mortified. Her tell came in the form of her chin quivering. Eyes straight ahead, she refused to look directly at him.

Telling her that he understood would do no good. So, he excused himself to head across the hall.

Carys was already pulling out the items. She held them out. "Here you go."

Damned if he didn't have to fight himself to keep from kissing her again.

Standing in a bedroom alone with Blaize shouldn't have been the most intimate moment she'd had in too long. But it was.

As Carys handed over the clothing, their fingers grazed. An electric jolt shocked her, sending volts shooting through her hand, her wrist, up her arm. Warming her. Blaize was pure sex. Everything about him was perfection. Like how his hands were calloused and rough but surprisingly tender to the touch.

He stood there for a moment like he was trying to process what had just happened, too.

And then he turned and walked out, hanging his head low. Shame?

She hoped he didn't feel remorse for the attraction that was happening between them. Hadn't she read something about survivor's guilt in cases like his? She remembered the person could feel guilty for secretly being glad their loved one's pain was over. Could meeting someone trigger more guilt? Sharing a kiss?

It dawned on her that theirs might have been the first one since losing his wife.

Rather than try to figure out what someone else was thinking, she moved next door to where she'd left a sleeping Rue.

Carys climbed underneath the covers, closed her eyes, and then crashed.

By the time she opened her eyes again hours later, sun filtered through the slats in the mini blinds. How long had she been asleep?

She immediately sat up to check on Rue. The baby's carrier was gone, the baby gone with it.

A moment of panic slammed into her. The door was

closed. She threw the covers off and opened it before stepping into the hall and listening.

The low hum of voices drifted toward her from the kitchen. There was not a peep from Rue.

Carys headed straight toward the bathroom, almost tripped over the neatly folded clothes at her feet. What was this? She picked them up. Her clothes? Washed, dried, and folded?

She headed into the bathroom, used the facilities, and cleaned up before dressing. A toothbrush had been laid out for her, along with toothpaste. Basically, heaven.

As soon as she dressed, she moved to the kitchen. The smell of fresh brew hit her senses from halfway down the hall. Her stomach growled. She couldn't remember the last time she'd slept so deeply or woken up so starved.

Rounding the corner to the kitchen, her heart skipped a couple of beats. She stopped, put a hand on the wall to steady herself. Seeing Blaize hold Rue while he talked quietly with an adoring grandmother caused her ovaries to squeeze. It would be helpful if the man could be more of a jerk.

"Morning," she said as she walked into the room.

"Morning to you," Blaize said with a smile that released half a dozen butterflies in her stomach. He had on jeans and a black T-shirt.

"Hello," Kit practically chirped. Her mood had drastically improved. "Grab some coffee and come sit with us."

Carys wasn't so sure that was a good idea. It felt a little too much like a family scene. Considering her background, she would probably say or do something to mess it up. Plus, she needed to get her CPS agent hat back on.

"Mind if I talk a walk first?" she asked, stalling for time so she could come up with a better reason. The last thing she wanted to do was hurt Kit's feelings. The woman had been nothing but welcoming and kind.

Blaize shot a look. The reason dawned on her. He didn't think it was safe for her to be outside alone. He stood up and gently handed Rue over to Kit.

"Finally my turn with this sweet little girl." Kit beamed.

"I'll go with you," he said.

She knew better than to argue if she wanted to stretch her legs to counter all the sitting she'd done yesterday. Normally, she would go on a run in the morning, but she didn't know the area. A walk was more manageable. How lost could she get?

Of course, Blaize would know the area.

"One sec," he said before leaving the room. When he came back, he had a gun tucked inside a waist holster that was clipped onto his jeans. The reminder of the danger they were in sobered her. "Ready?"

As much as she'd ever be.

"Let's go," she said, leading the way out the back door.

Once outside, she saw paint cans scattered around the back of the house.

"They might have been the cause of the noise last night," Blaize said after following her gaze. "Could have been a raccoon trying to climb them or searching for food."

"Makes sense."

They walked quietly for a while.

"I tried to find her last night and came up empty," he said. "Stephanie Cross isn't on social media that I could find, but that could be a married name."

"You don't remember anyone named Stephanie?"

"No."

They walked around the perimeter of the yard. A cool breeze caused her to shiver. If the weather dipped below seventy-five degrees, she threw on a sweater. Growing up in south Texas had a way of making you a wimp when it came to colder temperatures.

"Given it's Saturday, I'm at a loss as to getting more information about her," she said. "I'm waiting on the sheriff's report, but with the...*conditions* of the crash, we might never get a positive ID."

"That doesn't leave Rue in limbo?"

"It would only matter if a parent claimed her, which I was hoping you would do, but since you admitted to not having sex during that time Rue's status is up in the air."

"What if I just let it ride?"

"You mean keep her?" she asked, not hiding her shock. "You would do that?"

"Do you have a better idea?"

After the way she'd seen him with Rue this morning, it was a thought. She'd already bent the rules in this case. Could she look the other way on something as big as paternity?

No. Now what?

Chapter Eight

"I wish I could, but—"

Blaize put a hand up to stop Carys from finishing her sentence. "It was the first thing that popped into my mind. Forget I said it."

"I thought it was noble," she said, cracking another layer of ice that encased his heart. At this rate, he'd have no defense left before the weekend was over. "And very sweet."

"I'm not sweet." If only she knew what a jerk he could be. She would change her mind faster than a spring hailstorm tore through a town.

Carys smiled. "Fair enough."

"What will happen to her?"

"The orphanage." She frowned. "It's not a terrible place, but it is understaffed at the moment and I hate the thought of someone so little falling through the cracks." She was quick to add, "They wouldn't do it on purpose. Their mission is good, and they try to do their best. There are some out there I wouldn't trust as far as I could throw. This isn't one of those."

"They can't find good people?"

"Not enough for the demand."

"There has to be another way." He couldn't stand the

thought of Rue spending a night at the orphanage. The little girl perked Kit up, too. "Adoption?"

"You?"

Blaize shook his head. "Right. Bad idea. I have to figure out a way to turn this place around. Money is tight, and I can't let Kit lose her home, no matter what else happens. I might need to hire someone to look after her while I work on getting the ranch back in order, which will use up what little money I have left. I was hoping my brothers would answer my calls, but it's been crickets from them so far."

He didn't normally talk so much. Talking to Carys came as naturally as honey to a bee. He didn't have to force words. It was a nice change. When Lynn was in a good place, talking came easier, but it was nowhere near this easy. Carys had a way about her that made him want to open up.

Damned if he could figure out why.

"Did you get into a fight?" She cocked her head to one side.

"I pushed everyone away when Lynn first got sick. Even before that, if I'm honest. I told myself I was protecting her. She had bipolar disorder and wouldn't have wanted anyone to see her darker sides."

"That must have been hell."

"She was a trouper," he said.

Carys's eyebrow flew up. "I meant for you."

"You can't do that. You can't go there on the self-pity thing." It was a downward spiral that led to nowhere good. He knew firsthand.

"I'm not trying to come off as patronizing, but when do you ever prioritize your needs?"

Those words struck like an arrow to the center of his chest. Bull's-eye.

He tried to laugh it off. "I've never minded taking care of someone else."

"You're the oldest in your family, aren't you?"

"Yes, but what does that have to do with anything?" He was genuinely perplexed.

"I read this article about birth order and how it affects someone's personality," she said. "I'd say you're a classic firstborn."

"Because?"

"You take care of everyone else because you're used to being put in charge." Her tone wasn't accusing or coming off as judging, just factual. "You have two brothers, correct?"

"That's right."

"So, the middle one is likely the negotiator and the youngest—well, everyone always caters to the baby," she said. "They usually grow up with the most freedom and know how to push the envelope."

"No one was catered to by Cormac," he corrected.

"These are loose definitions." She studied him. "Do you disagree with the assessments? There's supposedly a ton of research out there on the subject."

"Raiden is the middle child of the family, and I can see where he is the peacemaker or the negotiator," Blaize said. "Or, at least, when he *was* talking to me. Growing up, he was the one who stepped in between our younger brother and me when there was an argument." He cracked a smile. "I was always right, of course."

She smiled right back. "Goes without saying."

"Raiden certainly kept a calm demeanor when I butted heads with Cormac," he said. "Which was probably more often that it should have been."

"And the youngest?"

"Phoenix definitely got the wild-child gene, but nothing like our father. Phoenix marches to his own drum and never cared what anyone else thought about him. He's grown now, but he sure ran with the wild mustangs, if you will, when we were younger. Not party-boy wild. More like a wild horse that didn't want to be tamed. In fact, there was a stint when we thought he would run off to join the rodeo." He thought about how different their mothers were. "All three of us come from different relationships, so I'm sure that influenced our personalities as well."

"You're how many years apart?"

"There's two years between Raiden and me, then one between him and Phoenix." Cormac was clearly "busy" in his younger days. Busy being a jerk who treated women like they were expendable. Blaize had learned how not to treat the opposite sex by watching dear old dad.

"Yikes."

"Yep." That was Cormac. "Classy, right?"

"It's hard to forgive your parents, isn't it?" Carys asked after a thoughtful pause. "They're human, and you kind of remember that. But they can hurt you the most out of anyone else, and their actions shape you for better or worse."

This sounded like more admission and commiseration than a comment about his life.

"It is next to impossible to forgive the bad ones," he said. "No one expects them to be perfect. Not as adults anyway. I've seen it done right. Take Kit, for example."

"She is close to perfection."

He smiled. "I would agree there."

"And easy to love."

"It's strange how her son came out so opposite," he said. "All Cormac cared about was a good party. I'm still scratching my head as to why my grandfather left him the responsibility of the ranch."

"Do you think it's possible your grandfather believed his son might change with the right amount of responsibility or motivation? Grow into the role?"

"It's hard to know what the man's thoughts were. He was the silent type. We always knew he loved us, even though I can't recall ever hearing him say the words. It was just his way. He did things like help Kit make our lunches before heading out for a long day working cattle. Or check in with us at night after we were ready for bed to ask if we'd eaten. We had and he knew the dinner routine. It was his way of making sure we knew he cared."

"Kit is so outgoing," Carys said. "Guess it is true what they say about opposites attracting."

He barked out a laugh at that one. It had been true in his marriage. He'd been the steady stream while Lynn had taken the roll of hurricane. "That's not always a positive."

"I hear you," she said, surprising him with her honesty. "I dated someone I thought was smart, maybe almost too smart, and he became clingy. Thought we were in a serious relationship when we weren't. I gave his name to the sheriff when he asked, but I haven't seen or heard from James in a couple of months."

"What do you mean by clingy?" He had no right to be jealous of her ex. Yet there was an undeniable twinge.

"I would turn the aisle at a grocery store and he'd be at the other end, hiding and spying," she said. "He wasn't good at it. Other times he'd suddenly be standing beside me while I was distracted looking in the meat case. Used to freak me right out."

"Did you file a complaint with the law?"

"No." She shook her head. "He never tried to harm me

or attack me in any way. Just left a rose on top of the hood of my car. Or a note saying he missed me and wanted to see me again. Small things like that, along with being in the same place at the same time. All of it used to creep me out. When someone says no, they mean no."

"Some people need to be taught the meaning of that word."

Blaize didn't like the sound of this one bit. James might have been stewing in his anger, plotting, over these past weeks. And now, what? He showed up during a storm because he'd been watching her house? It was plausible. At least the sheriff had James's name now. The man could be investigated and vetted. The sheriff would want to know if James had an alibi for yesterday.

Maybe Blaize could do a little more digging into James's background now that he had a name to work with and possibly a motive.

Carys's gaze shifted to the right, focused on something. A worry line creased her forehead.

"What is it?" he asked.

"I'm not sure, but I intend to find out," she said, starting in the direction of the object that had her concerned.

CARYS SAW A glint of metal on the ground in the tree line. She didn't want to get too ahead of herself, but it looked like it could be some kind of sharp object. A blade of some kind. A weapon?

Fear that the person from last night had tracked her here and came to spy on her was all-consuming. Could it be James? Would he have followed her here to the ranch? Knowing him, he would say that he was trying to protect her since she'd gone out into the storm, that he was following her just in case she needed him. Wasn't that a line he'd used before?

Her skin felt like dozens of fire ants had been let loose on it as she neared the object, realized it was a grill fork. It had a long handle and two sharp, sturdy prongs.

The image of her or Blaize being stabbed with it stamped her thoughts, causing icy fingers to grip her spine.

Blaize glanced over at the barbecue pit and back.

"This could do a lot of damage to someone if they were stabbed with it," she said to him. She searched her memory bank to remember when the kiss had happened versus the crashing sound outside. The kiss came first. She was certain. The thought that James, or some other creep, could have been watching through a window was enough to add a dozen more fire ants biting her skin.

"It sure could," Blaize said. "The raccoon theory is losing its appeal."

She picked up a stick and then used it to scoop up the grill fork by the small leather strap. "I seriously doubt the sheriff will be able to lift any usable DNA or prints after the storm we had. Still, I'd like to hold on to this."

"We can't be sure anyone was even here," Blaize said. He was right. She glanced around. The ranch was in need of serious TLC. "But we can try."

Carys nodded. And then something dawned on her. "Isn't this a cattle ranch?"

"Yes."

"Where's the cattle?" She looked around, surveying the land.

"They aren't here," he said. "But you figured that out already. A neighbor came over and took all of them so we could sort out Cormac's affairs and get Kit settled."

"That's nice of them."

"It's the way ranchers work. It's ingrained to help each other out. I still don't know how all this skipped a generation with Cormac. But my grandfather was a good person and never hesitated to lend a helping hand if someone needed him. People love Kit."

"I can see why," she said. "Where I used to live, the big push was to keep the place weird. But no one showed up in your time of need, if you know what I mean."

"Austin can be fun," he said with a laugh. She liked his smile and the way his eyes lit up and how the change in conversation broke some of the tension tightening her chest. "Do they still sell those *Keep Austin Weird* T-shirts?"

"Yes. Everywhere. If anything, people have doubled down." They were sold at coffee shops, gas stations, and street corners.

"Sounds about right for Austin. It's more of a vibe than a city. Good music. After Lynn died, I would drive in and hit up a few places on the regular."

Carys made a mental note to check with bartenders once they got a positive ID on Stephanie Cross. There had to be a picture of her somewhere they could take around to find out how she might have come into contact with Blaize.

"Speaking of weird, it's strange that someone I can't remember and am certain I don't know would put my name on her child's birth certificate." His tone was serious, matching the intensity of his gaze. "But these are strange times."

"I can think of a few reasons." None that she wanted to say out loud. He was kind, if rough around the edges. He would make a great dad. Was someone banking on the fact he wouldn't remember if they'd slept together or not? Hedging a bet that he would treat her child like a princess if he believed the girl was also his? Or that because of his kindness, her daughter would be safer with him if something happened to her?

Questions and speculation swirled with no easy answers.

"Are you going to explain that comment, or do I have to guess?" he asked, his tone lighter.

"I saw you with Rue earlier. Speaking of which, we should probably go inside," she said, needing time to let those thoughts seed. "And my brain won't work much longer without caffeine. Or breakfast, for that matter. And a glass of water sounds good, too." Using the stick, she set the grill fork down. "This is useless, isn't it?"

"Yes." He confirmed what she already suspected. The heavy rains would have washed away any evidence. If, in fact, anyone had been out there. The racoon really was the most likely culprit. Her imagination was running wild after the incident with her vehicle. "Oh, and I need to get to my car soon so I can survey the damage in the daylight."

Blaize's smile faded. And she hated being the one to put the frown on his face.

Chapter Nine

Blaize called the sheriff for the second time in two days. Standing at Carys's vehicle, he couldn't help but wonder if someone was listening in on her conversations or tracking her by phone. "Did you talk to anyone and tell them about your plans to come here before you came out to see me with Rue yesterday?"

"Um, no. Why?" She walked around her four-door sedan, assessing the damage.

She gasped and caught his stare before he could respond.

"You're saying someone might be listening in on my calls and conversations, aren't you?" she asked.

"I'm exploring all possibilities."

She paused, seemingly to regain her bearings after the realization. "Well, let's see, I had a conversation with one of my co-workers about not wanting to take Rue to Sister's Love," she said. "Harrison is his name."

"When the sheriff drops by to pick up the barbecue fork, you might want to give him the name," he said, then watched as half a dozen emotions passed over her face and behind her eyes. There was confusion, sadness, frustration, and a couple others before resignation.

"I seriously doubt Harrison would follow me," she said. "Or want to hurt me in any way."

"He might be fixated on you."

"You think?" Her face puckered. She shook her head as though physically rejecting the idea. "No… I mean, he was complaining about Rue crying and wanted me to get her out of the office because he said…"

Another gasp.

"He said the walls were paper thin," she said.

"Meaning he could be listening to your calls all day, personal and private."

"Even if he was, what would he have to gain by attacking me last night?" Her gaze unfocused like she was looking inside herself for the answer.

"Has he ever asked you out?"

"Harrison? No," she quickly said. "I'm pretty certain that I annoy him. Also, I've always thought he wasn't interested in women."

"Do you know much about his private life?"

"Well, to be honest, not really. No. Huh." She stood there for a long moment. "I guess we made small talk at the office. *How many cases are you working? Did you have a good weekend?* That type of surface-level conversation. He never asked me out on a date or even to grab a drink after work."

"Doesn't mean he isn't harboring feelings," he said. Another stab of jealousy landed.

"You're right, I guess." Her face scrunched again. "I'm just not seeing it. You usually know when someone is interested in you. I guess I never got that vibe from Harrison."

Coming from his perspective, Blaize agreed. When he was interested in someone, he made his intentions clear. Dating. Damn. He could only imagine how much rituals had changed since the last time he was in the dating pool. Folks used apps back in his day, but they seemed a whole lot more prevalent now. He'd also heard tell of folks getting tired of them. Something about app fatigue. It was understandable. You both swiped. You started a chat. Someone ghosted. Rinse. Repeat.

Lynn had been the first person he met on an app. Both stopped talking to other people shortly after. Three years later, he asked her to marry him. So, he didn't have a lot of experience to draw from.

Carys walked the perimeter of her vehicle, assessing the damage while he checked the area for any possible footprints. The chances he'd find any were slim to none. Still, he checked. The person who'd dropped the barbecue fork was sloppy, an inexperienced criminal.

The tree trunk lying across the road would have been too planned for someone like that. Right?

Or had the person intended to stop her so they could ambush her all along? Someone would have had to drive out here, move the trunk onto the road, and then what? Wait? The position of the log made it next to impossible to drive around. Was it random? Placed there?

Any tire tracks were washed away at this point. The heavy rain did a great job of erasing evidence. Was that calculated on the attacker's part? Had this person been waiting, biding his time?

And what, if any, links could there be to Stephanie Cross?

"Let me hop in and start the engine," she said. "Then I'll help you move the log."

He nodded. The parched earth soaked up most of the rain, so driving on mud wouldn't be an issue.

The vehicle started up. Carys didn't smile. She looked relieved.

The stalker theory was gaining steam in his mind. Could

be James or Harrison. Or the two other names she'd mentioned to the law. He needed to ask her about the others and what role they might play in her life.

"We should head back soon," he said to her as she exited the vehicle. "Kit and Rue were taking a nap when we left, but you never know when one will wake up."

"True," she said. "And you still haven't gotten any sleep."

"I power napped."

"It's not the same thing." She shot him a warning look that told him not to argue. It made him laugh.

It had been a long time since someone had been concerned about him. The nurses handed over pamphlets with support group names and numbers on them. He'd shot down their concerns, saying he was fine. Saying that he could handle it. Taking care of his wife was not a strain since Lynn was the one suffering. All he wanted to do was be there for her to make the road easier. Funny. You never really thought they were going to die. You held out unrealistic hope that a miracle cure would happen. You held on to stories of others who were knocking on death's door suddenly cured and back to a normal life, as if anything after an experience like this could go back to normal. And you held on to that hope until they took their last breath.

Then you sat in your disbelief when they were gone.

"Everything okay?" Carys asked. She'd walked up beside him.

"Fine."

"You sure about that?" Her left eyebrow arched.

"Do I seem like I'm not okay?" he snapped, realizing his tone came out a helluva lot harsher than intended. He put a hand up to stop her from responding. "I didn't mean that."

"I know." She folded her arms and leaned her hip against

the car. "And I realize we have to get back to the house as soon as possible. But…do you want to talk about it?"

Did he?

Could he?

Blaize let out a sharp sigh. "If I did talk about it… I'd want it to be with you."

She took a tentative step toward him. "I'm right here, Blaize. And it's okay to still be hurting."

He exhaled, slower this time.

She came closer and then reached for his wrists. Then she took a final step, closing the gap between them. "Is it okay if I touch you?"

"Yes." Damned if he wasn't falling down a rabbit hole with Carys. Would he recover this time?

CARYS TOOK BLAIZE'S wrists in her hands and then positioned his arms around her body. This close, she breathed in his spicy, dark-roast scent. She locked their gazes, searching his eyes to make sure that she wasn't overstepping her bounds. Touching him sent electrical impulses racing through her body. Her breath quickened.

"I've been thinking a lot about the kiss from yesterday," he said, his voice low and gravelly with something that sounded a whole lot like need. And something else. Regret?

"And?" She flinched, preparing for the worst.

"You're the first person I've kissed since…"

Carys sure as hell wasn't expecting those words. An ache formed low in her belly. Her fingers itched to outline every muscle on his beautiful body. A small smile toyed with the corners of her lips at thinking of him in terms of being beautiful. He wouldn't see it that way even though he had those hard planes and angles down pat. His jawline could crack concrete. He would laugh at those descriptions, too. And those full lips over straight, white teeth. Warmth pooled between her thighs.

"I'm honored," she finally said. Her throat suddenly dried, so she swallowed to ease some of it. Did he regret it? "I hope it didn't disappoint."

His tongue slicked across his bottom lip. She stared at the silky trail it left behind.

"I know we agreed it shouldn't happen again, but I would very much like to ask your permission to kiss you one more time."

Standing this close, her body craved more of his touch. Kissing him complicated matters, but she was tired of refusing to give her body what it desperately wanted and needed…to be touched by Blaize.

Her only hesitation was that she knew one time wouldn't be enough.

Could she pull back at this point?

A nearby rustling of leaves made the decision for her. Both of their attention snapped to the sound. Blaize took a step in front of her, placing his body in between her and the noise, forming a human shield.

Their movement caused a squirrel to bolt across the street. They stood there for a long moment, waiting, watching.

"That was not a smart move on my part," Blaize said, shame in his tone.

"I did that, Blaize. Not you." She noticed his habit of blaming himself every time something went wrong. An eldest-child fault? Or did he blame himself in some way for his wife's death? "If you ever want to talk about it, I'm here."

"For how long?" he asked, his tone so low she almost didn't hear him.

"I'm right here," she said in the most reassuring tone possible. After what he'd been through, it wouldn't surprise her if he was afraid deep down to get close to anyone for fear of losing them. That fear would bubble to the surface in comments like the one he just made.

He surveyed the area. His muscles were so tense if they were cords they would have snapped by now.

"Do you want to sit in my car for a few minutes before we drive back?" she asked.

"Let's move this barrier first."

With both of them working, it took all of five minutes to clear the road.

He walked over to the driver's side and opened the door for her. She took a seat. Blaize rounded the front of the vehicle before settling in the passenger side. She rolled the windows down a crack. Just enough to keep fresh air flowing, while making it easier to hear if someone came up to surprise them.

Blaize kept his gaze focused on the stretch of road in front of them. They sat there, quiet, for a long moment. Pushing him to speak would only cause him to withdraw further. In her two years on the job, she'd witnessed people who experienced trauma. They needed space. They needed a gentle nudge.

He was a good person, someone who took care of everyone around him without asking anything in return. It might not have been her job to help him, but she could be there for him. She could lend an ear. But only if he wanted to take that step.

She'd also learned on the job that she couldn't fix other people. They had to want to fix themselves.

"Holding my wife's hand while she faded was the hardest thing I'll ever be asked to do," he said.

"I have nothing to compare it to," she said quietly, reverently. "And I can't begin to fathom how that would feel."

"There was so much medication by the end," he said. "She was doped up all the time to stay out of pain. One night, the lights were low. I sat next to her, head down, eyes on the phone. And I missed it. I had a work email that I was writing a response to. She said my name a few minutes earlier, and I just kept staring at the screen. Held my finger up to tell her that I'd be with her in a second. By the time I looked up, she was gone."

Damn.

Carys exhaled a slow breath as the weight of those words descended around her, cloaked her. The amount of guilt he carried around made even more sense now.

"You were by her side," she said to him. "That would matter the most."

"What did she want to say to me?" he asked slowly. "What did I miss? Was she in pain? Was there something I could have done to ease it? To help? Did she need something from me? Or did she want to tell me that she loved me one more time, and I robbed both of us of the pleasure of hearing those words out loud?"

Carys didn't respond. Those questions were rhetorical. It was him thinking out loud. Needing to say those words to someone.

"I spent so much time with her and missed the most important moment of her life." He was beating himself up. Words of encouragement wouldn't help right now, so she tucked them away for when he might be ready to hear them.

Reality nailed her.

Once Rue was settled wherever she was supposed to be, Carys and Blaize would likely lose contact. They lived in two different worlds, and he had the responsibility of turning the ranch around along with the self-imposed duty of taking care of Kit for the rest of her life.

She hoped his grandmother would be around for a very long time. Kit was wonderful. And yet Carys wished Blaize could have time to heal from taking care of his wife. It was obvious he loved her. And no matter how strong the attraction was between Carys and Blaize, she would never be able to compete with a ghost.

An emptiness she'd never experienced before filled her chest, and suddenly all the oxygen sucked out of the vehicle.

Chapter Ten

Blaize never talked about Lynn. He thought about her every day, almost every minute of every day. But he didn't talk about her.

Until now.

Saying those words out loud chipped some of the thousand-pound weight off his shoulders.

"Ever notice how we're always harder on ourselves than we are on other people?" Carys asked.

He nodded. She'd been quiet.

"If you knew someone going through what you just described, someone who was being a dying person's sole support…what would you say to them?" she asked.

"I'd tell them to do the best they could and savor each moment," he said. "I'd tell them to try to find humor together in small things. And I'd remind them to take care of themselves, too." It dawned on him why she'd asked the question as he heard his own response. "And you're wondering why I don't give myself that same advice."

"No," she said. "Just observing how hard we are on ourselves and how much softer we are on others, especially when someone we care about is going through hell."

He barked a laugh. Yes. He could relate. "I'm still not letting myself off the hook."

"You don't have to," she said. "No judgment here."

Blaize sat there for a long moment, letting those words really sink in. They'd been gone for a while, longer than he intended. "We should really get back to Kit and the baby."

"Okay."

He didn't realize he'd tensed up so much before her response until he exhaled. With Lynn, almost everything became a challenge or an outright fight. Carys's demeanor had a calming effect on people, on him. Even when they stood close and his body was an exploding minefield of electricity and need, he felt a sense of peace that was foreign.

Growing up in a battleground with Cormac, then with Lynn's bipolar disorder, he'd gotten used to always being ready for a fight.

Carys drove them to the house since the damage on her car was thankfully just cosmetic. Frustrating as all hell, but nothing a good dent-repair shop couldn't handle. Mechanically, the car was sound. Tires were good. He'd half feared the attacker would return and rupture them. Too risky?

Damned if he wasn't already thinking about the kiss from yesterday again. How it was unlike any others.

They pulled up. Carys parked next to his Jeep. Both vehicles could use a good hosing off.

"I can find someone to fix the damage to your vehicle," he said after opening her door for her. It looked as though someone had taken a baseball bat to it.

"Thanks, but I can look up a place just as easy." She held out her phone. "You can find almost anything on one of these."

"And have it delivered," he joked. "Just not out here."

"Leaving the city was definitely an adjustment," she said.

"Why did you come all the way out here to Maverick Pass?" He opened the back door for her after unlocking it.

"For a job. They aren't exactly easy to get."

"Austin can be a tough place to find work, but the medical options are standout," he said. There would come a day when he didn't know who the best bipolar doctor was or bone-cancer specialist. A year had passed since Lynn's death, and he still checked his calendar for appointments out of habit.

"The job market was brutal, even for the kind of work I do."

They entered the kitchen. He listened for sounds coming from the bedroom. Kit had insisted on having Rue stay with her.

"Blaize!" Kit hollered.

And then the baby wound up and wailed.

Heart in his throat, he blew past Carys. The door was still locked, but this old house would be easy to break into. All the latches and locks were too old. Hell, the windows were ancient. No one expected crime all the way out here.

"Are you—"

He stopped midsentence the second he entered the doorway, rushed to Kit, who was lying on her side and curled into a ball.

"What happened?" he asked before taking a knee beside her. He scanned her for obvious signs of injury—blood or a bone sticking out through her skin. He couldn't find anything from this angle.

He could barely hear himself think over the crying baby. Carys was there in the next second, picking up the little girl and offering a soothing tone.

"I'll take her into the next room," she said before disappearing. Her voice might be calm, but panic was written all over her features.

"Can I help you sit up?" he asked Kit when the crying subsided.

"I think so," she said, issuing a frustrated grunt. "I was trying to get to the bathroom, and I lost my balance. Hit my head on the dresser."

"Where?" he asked as he wrapped an arm around her and gently guided her to sit up.

She leaned against the dresser as she brought her hand up to feel around the crown of her head. "Here." She took his hand and placed it on the spot.

A pump knot was already forming.

"We need to get you to the ER," he said, doing his level best to tamp down the panic rising in his chest.

"You'll do no such thing," Kit protested. "My name is Kit Wilde, short for Katherine." She rattled off a couple other facts to prove she was lucid. Facts like the day of the week, her birthday, and the address.

"Then at least allow me to grab an ice pack," he said. It could help with any pain.

"That I can live with." Kit smiled with that grandmotherly warmth in her eyes. "I'm sorry to be such a pain."

"You couldn't be."

"I've been thinking about what you said about Lynn. It couldn't have been easy on you, and I'm figuring you took care of your wife all by your lonesome."

He nodded, unsure where this was going.

"You shouldn't have to step in and take care of an old lady like me," she said. "It's time you live your life for yourself, Blaize. I mean it, and I believe the others will agree."

"Not a chance." There was no way Kit was leaving the home she'd built. He frowned. "Are you trying to kick me out?"

Kit laughed.

"Would you go?" she asked.

"Nah. Probably not." He smiled. "You raised me and my brothers. I may not have heard back from them yet, but I will. And they'll agree with me, by the way."

She folded her arms across her chest and pouted.

"What can I say? We love you, and it's your turn to be taken care of. And it's high time you reclaimed your bedroom." He shook his head. "I have no idea what Cormac was thinking, but if he was alive, I'd..." One look at her said he was hurting her feelings by insulting her son. "I'm sorry, Kit. What he's done to this place burns me up."

"You don't know what happened to Cormac to turn him that way."

What?

CARYS GAVE A self-satisfied smile after successfully changing a diaper and feeding Rue a bottle. Now the baby was happily stretching her hands out in front of her, cooing, and basically looking at this world like everything was miraculous. Carys couldn't remember the last time she felt that way about anything in life. As a child, she'd been suffocated, miserable. Taking charge of her life meant being cut off by her father, a choice no person should've had to make.

She exhaled a slow breath and refocused. It was Saturday, her day off from work. She could turn her phone off and not worry about her boss figuring out what she'd done. At least, not today. That would be Monday's problem, if it surfaced at all. Could she hide all this from work?

Relinquishing custody of a child to their parent was something Carys did on a regular basis. Technically, there was no proof that Blaize wasn't the biological father. Sure, a simple spit test would do the trick in a matter of hours, but she hadn't filed her report yet and so there was no reason for work to question that she'd done the right thing.

There were a few wrong things to worry about. For instance, staying overnight. That was out of the bounds of her job description and could be scrutinized should this case go to court. The storm could explain being stranded. Blaize offered shelter in said storm. The kiss they'd shared might be a bigger issue if questioned about developing a personal relationship with the father of her charge.

That would be the point the case could go south faster than a beginner skater on ice.

Wanting Blaize wasn't an issue. Her body craved his touch. She'd dreamt about his hands on her last night. The kiss they'd shared had been soul-defining. It also caused her to question what she knew about attraction. Had she been settling for partners who either couldn't commit to a relationship or were too clingy? Finding middle ground seemed impossible. Finding someone who saw her through Blaize's eyes seemed unthinkable. Finding someone who made her want things like a real love with a person who loved her back was unimaginable.

Keeping everyone at arm's length was her superpower. Who was she without it?

She listened for signs from the bedroom that Kit was all right. Seeing her lying on the floor, curled up on her side, had caused Carys's stress levels to shoot through the roof. The distraction of caring for Rue kept Carys's nerves at a level above panic.

Considering Carys never saw herself as the "get married and have kids" type, the satisfaction she got from calming the baby took her by surprise.

Maybe she could consider getting a cat? Or should start small with trying to keep a houseplant alive? The responsibility of day-to-day care would be different than her little win this afternoon.

All this was a distraction from her real purpose—finding Rue's birth father. To do that, she needed to know more about Stephanie Cross. Once Kit's status was confirmed as healthy, Carys could regroup with Blaize.

Hunger pangs got the best of her. She missed those days in Austin when she could just pull up an app on her phone and have food delivered to her door. It was expensive but worth every penny on days like this.

Living in Maverick Pass had honed her cooking skills. She could do more than butter toast, which was good. Thank the stars for online recipes and cooking tips. She would be lost without the internet. Didn't make her a true chef by any means. At least she could feed herself with relative ease. Eating at home had other benefits. She ate healthier.

A noise from the hallway drew her attention back to the present. Blaize walked into the kitchen.

One look at him had her standing up. "More coffee?"

"Yes, please." He rubbed the day-old scruff on his chin.

"Coming right up." She fixed two after settling Rue on the blanket placed on the floor.

Blaize's toe snagged the rain bucket, causing water to slosh and a few droplets to spill. He muttered a curse, glanced at Rue, and then apologized.

"Think she can understand you?" Carys handed over a fresh cup of black coffee.

"No," he said. "I don't want her to get used to those words. I'm convinced the subconscious picks up more than we realize, even in little ones. While around her, I want to do better with language."

The word *while* shouldn't hit hard. Its temporary nature reminded her just how short this visit would be. She needed to go home because there was no way she could sell staying with him over an entire weekend in court should it come to that.

"If Stephanie listed you as Rue's father and it's a blatant lie, she either doesn't know who he is or did and was keeping the baby from him for a reason," she said as they took seats at the kitchen table.

"My mind goes to some pretty dark places when it comes to keeping paternity from a father," he said.

"For instance?"

"Maybe she was being abused and didn't want that life for her daughter," he said. "Or the father was a criminal and she didn't want her daughter brought up in that lifestyle."

"Both are logical reasons." She took a sip of coffee. "Kids change people, don't they?"

"How so?"

She leaned her elbows against the table. "Stephanie could have been fine with a wild lifestyle before this little darling was born. During her pregnancy, she might have realized she needed to change. Rue deserves better. So, she hatched a plan to escape. She sneaks away before her boyfriend or husband, whatever the case may be, knows she's carrying his baby and then writes your name down on the birth certificate to throw him off the trail."

"If she really made a plan like this, it stands to reason she would change her identity, too."

"I should get a report on Monday," she said. "It's sad that her life was cut short after all that scheming and planning, not to mention she wouldn't have planned on leaving Rue an orphan."

"She's not an orphan," he said with finality. "If the father turns out to be a disaster like we think, we'll figure something else out. Stephanie Cross, the person who put my name on that birth certificate trusted me to do the right thing. I won't let her or Rue down."

Blaize was the most honorable person Carys had ever met. She understood why someone would choose him even though it wasn't fair to put him in that position. *You didn't expect to need him, did you, Stephanie?* A picture emerged of a desperate pregnant woman who needed to escape her situation and have a backup plan should the worst happen.

And the worst did happen.

"Are you hungry?" he asked after her stomach growled.

"Yes."

"We could head out to eat since there isn't much left here," he said.

Being seen out and about with Blaize and the baby would definitely not be a good move. But hiding made her feel like she was doing something wrong.

Was she?

Chapter Eleven

"I have a picture of Stephanie Cross."

The announcement caught Blaize off guard. He crossed the kitchen in a few quick strides to where Carys had been perched for the past hour on her laptop. Kit and the baby were resting before dinner, so he was alone with Carys.

"Does she look familiar?" She angled the screen toward him as he took the seat next to her. Their outer thighs brushed, causing electricity to pulse up his leg, his body's reaction to her amplified by the length of time it had been since he'd had sex. It was the only explanation that made sense. Blaize was no stranger to sex within the bounds of a relationship, but no one had stirred a reaction like this one.

He studied the screen. Kinky red hair. Too much makeup. Mole on her right cheek. The mole resonated, but she had on so much makeup it was hard to tell what features were hidden underneath the mask. "There is something familiar about her."

"Makeup can do wonders to change someone's appearance. She has used contouring makeup just about everywhere on her face. For instance, see here." She pointed to Stephanie's nose. "This is making her nose look thinner than it is."

"The hair is throwing me off."

"Looks like she has a perm, and it's possible she colored it. That doesn't look like a natural redhead."

"I'd have to see her in person to know for certain, which is clearly not possible under the circumstances."

"Well, no, but we could visit some of the bars you used to frequent in Austin and ask around. Maybe a bartender will know her and be able to provide a name," she said.

"What would we do with Rue?"

"Kit needs someone here for support in case she falls again," she said. "Maybe they can watch over Rue?"

"My grandmother might have someone who can step in for a day while we head to Austin," he said.

"Right. Ranchers are the rare breed who still watch out for each other. Too bad everyone isn't like that."

"Many of us still do." He thought about what Kit said to him earlier about not knowing what made Cormac turn out the way he had. If the man started out being a good human, it must have been something horrific to turn him into the person he became. Someone who'd lost touch with his roots, his humanity.

Did Blaize really want to know what happened? Would it do any good? You couldn't go back and change the past. He learned the lesson a long time ago. Didn't everyone have some kind of trauma in their background? There was no excuse for the way Cormac treated people.

"We should make a list of the bars you used to go to." Carys's voice cut into his heavy thoughts.

"That's easy. There were three—Deep Roots Bar, Peggie Hays, Chord Street Bar." He'd stopped off at a handful of others. Not long enough for someone to remember his name unless this Stephanie or whatever her name was figured out another way.

Nope. Not possible. He always used cash at bars. No

one needed to know his business, and credit cards could be traced. He didn't appreciate how easy it was to stalk someone online or memorize their habits. A determined criminal could get most everything they wanted to know about a person online.

With social media, folks volunteered personal information about their lives on an almost daily basis. Where they ate. What night was date night. What their family looked like. Where they went on vacation. What school their kids attended. Information was endless, which made Stephanie more interesting since there wasn't a profile for her anywhere near Maverick Pass or Austin.

Blaize had one too many a couple of times at bars. Not enough to sleep with a stranger, and especially not enough to sleep with a stranger and then forget it happened. He would have remembered. He hadn't kissed anyone in the past year except for Carys.

"When Kit wakes, I'll have her reach out to a neighbor to see if they can come sit with her and Rue. It's Saturday night, so the bars will be open late. We can make the drive and hit all three in one night if traffic obliges."

Carys glanced at the time on the computer. "We'll have to leave soon."

"I know."

The sound of gravel crunching underneath tires got Blaize up and moving to the window. He grabbed a knife on the way. It might've been the sheriff finally showing up to pick up the barbecue fork, but he couldn't be sure.

Nope.

He didn't recognize the dark blue pickup. The driver, on the other hand, was Raiden.

"Who is it?" Carys asked, walking up beside him.

"My brother." Blaize set the knife on the counter and

headed toward the back door. He didn't have the first clue if Raiden would be happy to see him. Time to find out and see if the damage done to their relationship could be repaired.

"Should I wait here in case Kit or Rue needs something?" Carys asked.

"Would you mind?" he asked. "I'm not sure what kind of reunion this is going to be. Might be better on both fronts if I go by myself to face my brother before introducing him to you."

"I'll be right here if you need me." She touched his arm as he walked past. The contact sent electrical impulses zinging through him. "You got this."

"Thank you," he said. Her gentle support seeded a sense of calm in a place deep inside him. Denying it wouldn't make it any less true.

Raiden parked. He hopped out of the driver's seat and came flying at Blaize. He tensed up for a fight. Instead, his brother wrapped him in a bear hug.

"Hey, man. I'm so sorry about Lynn. I would have been there for you if I'd known," Raiden said. It dawned on Blaize that he wasn't the only one making calls to Raiden and Phoenix. Raiden must have had a conversation with Kit.

"There wasn't anything anyone else could do," Blaize said, embracing his brother.

"Bull hockey. We could have been your support system. Phoenix would have been there, too. We both feel like jerks for not taking your calls. Or, maybe I should say that I know he feels like a jerk since I haven't heard back from him." Maybe there was something to this birth-order bit. Raiden was being the go-between for Blaize and their youngest brother.

He cracked a smile. "You're here now. Kit needs all

three of us. This ranch needs all three of us if we're going to keep it in the family."

"I'm just here for the weekend, man. Came to tell you that Phoenix and I think we should dump this place," Raiden said.

Blaize took a step away from his brother. "You talked to each other without including me?"

"Not in the last forty-eight hours. The last time I spoke to our brother, we made a pact. Plus, you made your position clear, Blaize."

"And so you just left me out of the conversation altogether?" His temper was getting the best of him.

"That's why I'm here now," Raiden said. "That and to tell you how sorry I am."

"So, you'd toss Kit out on her ear? Make her lose the only home she's known for her entire adult life? The home she built?"

Raiden stood there, studying, listening. "You want to know the truth?" he asked.

"What kind of question is that? Of course I want to know the truth."

"Kit is the one who urged me to sell. Said you are being hardheaded and that I needed to find Phoenix so we could both show up and convince you to do the right thing and dump this…what did she call it…shanty."

Wait. What?

To say he felt blindsided was an understatement. What was Kit thinking?

"Said it was falling apart at the seams and that you, being you, wanted to fix it up for her but it's too much work, and we all have our own lives. Said she didn't want to get in the way."

"And you believed her?" Blaize asked, incredulous.

"She sounded sincere, man. What am I supposed to think? Kit is a firecracker and knows herself. Said she doesn't want to live in a place that's falling apart anymore."

Color Blaize confused. "Did she mention that she tripped and fell last night?"

Raiden shook his head.

"Hit her head on the dresser and ended up with a pump knot."

Raiden stood there, brows furrowed. He crossed his arms over his chest as he listened.

"She needs us more than ever, Raiden. Can you rightly see kicking her out of here?"

"The place needs a lot of work, Blaize."

"Nothing the three of us can't handle." Was he being overly optimistic? He didn't think so. It would take dedication and time.

"What about the financials?" Raiden asked.

"They are as bad as you think they might be."

"Kit said you'd try to talk me out of my stance," Raiden said. "She was one hundred percent right."

Why would Kit do that? Why would she push them to sell? It made no sense to Blaize. "I don't care what she said. Kit loves this place. Leaving here would be like losing her husband all over again."

"Did she tell you to sell?"

"Yes."

"Why don't you take her word for it?" Raiden asked. It was a reasonable question, and he didn't have a great answer.

"Can you honestly say that you believe her?"

"She was pretty convincing on the phone," he said. "I'm here to talk to you in person like we should have done when you first got Lynn's diagnosis. And I want to be able to look Kit in the eye when she argues her case."

There was more than a hint of doubt in Raiden's tone. Blaize could work with that. If his brother's mind was already made up, there would be no use discussing the subject further. One trait all three brothers inherited was a stubborn streak a mile long and stronger than a bull's.

"Why don't you come inside and have a cup of coffee," Blaize said. His plans to head to Austin tonight just tanked.

KIT WALKED INTO the kitchen and straight to the window. "Raiden is here. Good."

Carys wasn't so sure she liked the tone of Kit's voice. "Everything all right?"

"It is now," the older woman said, confusing her further.

Since she would find out what that meant soon enough, she rinsed out her coffee cup and set it in the sink.

Blaize followed his brother inside. The family resemblance showed in height and build. Raiden would be considered hot by most standards. His hair was a little longer, with wispy curls at the ends. In her opinion, Blaize was the best looking. No contest.

"I'm Raiden," he said to her after greeting Kit and giving his grandmother a warm hug. So far, the Wilde men were the most grounded she'd met in Maverick Pass. They were the hottest, too, but that was a different story.

"Carys," she said. "It's nice to meet you."

"My brother said you work for CPS," Raiden said.

"That's right."

"And that you brought a baby here believing she belonged to Blaize," he said.

She nodded. "Sure did."

"I'm sure you two will get to the bottom of it," he said.

"Thanks. I hope so." She glanced at Blaize. "Are we still good to head to Austin soon?"

"Now that my brother is here, I should probably not—"

"Go ahead," Kit insisted. "We'll be just fine."

"I don't know," Blaize said. Eyebrows drawn together combined with the worry line etched in his forehead told Carys he was seriously contemplating their next move.

"Is the kid here now?" Raiden glanced around the room.

"She's sleeping," Kit said.

"How hard can it be to watch over a little thing that sleeps most of the time?" he asked.

Carys laughed at the same time Blaize did, and equally hard.

"What?" Raiden asked.

"You have no idea until you know," Blaize said.

"Go and do what you need to do," Kit interjected. "We'll be fine. Isn't that right, Raiden?"

"We've got this," he confirmed.

"There's enough formula and diapers to last a couple of days," Carys supplied.

One look at Blaize said he'd made up his mind. He gave a slight nod as he locked gazes with Carys. Checking to see if she was on the same page?

"Let's do this." She could think of no better reason to put her job on the line than to help Rue find a real home. If going to Austin got them one step closer to that, so be it.

"I'll grab an overnight bag."

"Can we stop off at my place on the way out of town?" she asked. "I need a change of clothes."

"Sure," he said.

The thought of spending the night with Blaize in a hotel room should probably freak her right out. It didn't. Sure, the sexual current running between them showed no signs of dimming. However, they were adults capable of restraint. Her body wanted to argue against what her mind realized… having any type of relationship with Blaize beyond professional would shatter her once it ended.

"It was good to meet you," she said to Raiden as Blaize excused himself to grab his bag.

Raiden's gaze bounced from Carys to Kit and back. "I apologize if I'm stepping out of line here, but Blaize seems different with you around."

"Our relationship is strictly professional," she countered a little too quickly. Had she just showed her hand to Blaize's family? "I'm here because of Rue. Your brother has been great, though. And we're going to get to the bottom of paternity." Wow, had she really just rambled on?

Great. Way to keep cool.

"I understand," Raiden said with a layered look. "I'm sure the two of you will figure it out soon."

"In the meantime, I sure have enjoyed having another woman in the house," Kit interrupted. "I hope you'll stay on a little longer when you return from Austin." She glanced at Raiden. "Don't get me wrong—I love my boys. But the house can use more feminine energy."

Her smile lit up her eyes.

Carys laughed.

Blaize walked into the room. He stopped and studied everyone's faces. He opened his mouth to speak and then snapped it shut before focusing on Carys. "Ready?"

Probably not, but they needed to go anyway.

Chapter Twelve

Carys had been quiet on the ride to her apartment. Too quiet. Blaize had half a mind to ask what his family might have said to her. He decided to let it ride instead.

He parked on the street in front of her bungalow.

The crease in her forehead when she glanced at him concerned him.

"What's wrong?" he asked.

A beat passed. "Maybe nothing. I'm not sure. I think the trash can has been scooted closer to the window. I don't leave it there."

"Do you want to come with me to check it out or stay in the Jeep while I take a look?" he asked, reaching for the door handle.

"I'm coming." She was out the passenger side before he could open the door for her.

Carys took the lead as he scanned the area for any unusual activity.

The trash can had been pushed against the wall underneath what looked like a kitchen window. Nothing else seemed out of the ordinary. "The storm could have blown it over or tossed it down the street. A well-meaning neighbor might have returned it."

"That's a good point," she said. "Mind if we take a walk

around the house before going in? Just to be sure nothing else feels funny?"

"I'm right behind you." He was behind her and a little bit to the side so he could block her using his body should anything come flying at them. A stalker made more and more sense as they walked. She turned the second corner, looked at the window, and froze.

"The window is cracked open." She pointed. "See that?"

"I sure do," he said. "Do you ever leave them like that?"

"Not usually. I don't normally leave the house without checking."

"You had Rue with you. Right?" It was possible she might have forgotten.

"True." She shook her head. "I'm probably searching for something that just isn't there, you know? My mind is tuned to finding something because of the trash can. You're most likely right about it. The storms were fierce. It's highly likely the wind tossed it around while I was gone. It wouldn't be the first time that happened."

"We'll check every inch of the house before we let our guards down," he said.

"Sounds like a plan." She walked to the back door, opened it, and entered the kitchen. The place was simple, orderly, and clean. It looked like she put everything in its place with care. A *You Had Me at Merlot* dish towel was draped over the oven handle. Under different circumstances, he would have chuckled. Right now, he was focused on ensuring no one was hiding in a closet somewhere.

Room by room, he cleared the house. The bedroom window—the cracked one—was last. "No one is hiding here. I've checked every nook and cranny." That was the good news. Her unsettled feeling had him concerned. It was never a good idea to ignore intuition. "If someone was here, they're gone now." He stopped short of saying they were safe. "Does anything look out of place?"

The living room consisted of a small sofa with a matching chair, a coffee table with a book on top, and a side table with a lamp. A blanket had been tossed onto the couch, and the pillows were messy. It looked like someone had been sitting here, relaxing, and then had to get up in a hurry with no time to straighten up. The Rue effect?

"I don't remember. It's hard to say. Everything is usually in its place, but having a little one around really changes things."

He let himself smirk—Rue effect.

"All I could think about was her and how pitiful she sounded," she said. "Hearing a baby cry and being helpless to stop it is the worst possible feeling in the world."

"Agreed."

"I'll just grab a few things, and we can head out," she said before disappearing through a doorway in between the living and dining room.

"Okay." He took a step and heard a rattle. He withdrew his foot as though a snake bit him. A memory punched him. Damned if he hadn't suppressed it until now. Until looking down and seeing the baby's rattle on the carpet. He bent over and picked it up, studied it. Moisture pooled in his eyes. He'd been so focused on Lynn that he'd forced the memory out of his mind, pushed it down somewhere deep where it couldn't surface without the right trigger.

"Hey." Carys's voice caught him off guard. He didn't realize that she'd walked back into the room.

Blaize grunted, set the toy on top of the coffee table, and then headed toward the front door. "Lock up so we can get on the road."

He didn't look back. Didn't want her to see the emotion pooling in his eyes, threatening to spill over.

Dammit.

Blaize walked right past Carys, not stopping until he was seated on the driver's side of his Jeep. He turned the engine on, and waited. She took a few minutes to appear. For a second, he wondered if he'd offended her.

When she set her bag in the back seat, she didn't make eye contact. Her demeanor was calm. Too calm? Part of him wanted her to get mad. Hell, cuss him out.

Instead, she took the passenger seat and said, "Ready when you are."

He banked a U-turn after setting the GPS toward Austin.

They drove for a while before she cleared her throat and asked, "What about the baby's rattle upset you?"

"Nothing."

"You don't have to tell me," she said. "I've been picking up on something…call it a vibe. And it's been causing me to wonder how you feel about starting a family."

"What do you mean?"

"The way you look at Rue when no one is watching," she said.

Blaize clamped his mouth shut rather than bite out a retort. She was spot-on with her observation. The rattle dislodged a memory. One he'd been holding in for a long time. Too long?

Opening up felt like cutting open a vein. Stuffing it down felt like a time bomb waiting to explode.

"Have I mentioned Lynn had bipolar disorder?"

"You have."

"Right." *Here goes…*

"She was pregnant once," he said. "She showed me one of those home pregnancy tests."

"What happened?"

"I was thrilled when I saw the result," he said. "For some reason, a rattle just like Rue's came to mind. It was the first thing I wanted to buy. But Lynn started crying, and they weren't exactly happy tears. She unraveled, said she needed to stay with a friend to clear her head."

"That must have been hard for you, and her."

"It was. She shut me out during a difficult time for both of us."

"What happened?"

"Lynn turned up three days later. I came home from work to find her sitting on the couch drinking wine straight from the bottle." The memory threatened to burn a hole in his chest. Talking about it tamped down some of the blaze. "Said all the stress must have made her lose the pregnancy but that she was relieved because she didn't want kids with me anyway.

"I lost it," he said. "I'm not proud of my actions, but my temper got the best of me. I said words that I wish I could take back." Guilt punched him again like it happened yesterday.

"I'm sorry, Blaize. For both of you." A few beats passed. "Did she say why? You obviously wanted the child. Had you ever talked about having a family with her?"

"Yes," he said. "We wanted kids, or so I thought. She said the possibility of carrying a child woke her up to the fact she didn't actually want kids. Before that, she'd wanted two, a boy and a girl. I didn't care. She said she couldn't risk passing on the disorder to children. Said it wouldn't be fair to them or to me. Said she was enough of a hot mess without adding to the equation."

"I bet that was hard to hear from someone you loved so much."

"It was." He could admit that much. "So, if you catch me looking at Rue and thinking about what might have been, you're probably catching a weak moment."

"That's not weak, Blaize. You are the strongest person I know." She reached over and touched his hand, sending warmth spreading through him. "The more I get to know you, the more respect I have for you. Life hasn't been easy. Has it?"

"I never expected easy," he said. "I'd hoped for fair instead."

CARYS DIDN'T WANT to like Blaize more than she already did. She was already treading dangerous waters, barely keeping her head above water when it came to the man. His raw honesty wasn't helping her keep an emotional distance.

"Fair isn't always on the table, is it?" she asked.

"We've talked too much about me. What about you?" He turned the tables. "You lost your mother at a young age."

"That's right. I already shared that with you." Where did she begin with her other parental relationship? "As far as my father is concerned, we haven't spoken more than two words in six years. He cut me off when we disagreed about my future. Told me to go away and not worry about coming back. That he no longer had a daughter."

"That's harsh. You didn't deserve that."

"No one does," she agreed. "I get that he was hurting after my mom died. But his reaction made it like losing two parents in one blow. You know?"

"I can see that."

"Losing her caused him to double down on protecting me. His grip was so tight, I was tempted to rebel. I didn't. I guess it made me want to help others even more, especially kids."

It made her think about Rue. "What's going to happen to that little girl back at your house if her father turns out to be a criminal? Or if we never uncover his identity? The courts would never give her to me. Plus, I wouldn't know the first thing about taking care of a baby full time. I was an only child. And I might have had responsibilities around the house, but I was never responsible for a human life. I've never even kept a plant alive. I don't even want children, which is part of the reason I chose this profession. I can help them without the day in, day out responsibility that I have no idea if I'll ever be ready for."

"Parents do a real number on kids sometimes, don't they?" It was a rhetorical question.

"Thank you for listening," she said after catching her breath. "And not judging me or telling me that I'm supposed to want kids and a family."

"Why would I do that?" he asked with genuine care and authenticity in his voice.

She shrugged. "Isn't it supposed to be natural to want to have a baby?"

"Every person has a right and responsibility to make that decision for themselves."

"I couldn't agree more." Since most of the trip had been heavy with conversation, she changed course. "You know what sounds good right now to me?"

"What's that?"

"Ice cream."

Blaize laughed. "How about Amy's Ice Cream?"

"Is there a better place?"

"Not as long as Mexican Vanilla is on the menu," he said. She appreciated him going with the flow. Talking to him was a little too easy, and she needed to pull back before the connection deepened. She was already swimming in new territory and needed to get her sea legs.

The very real threat of being sucked out by a strong current and drowned slammed into her. As much as her heart wanted to lean into Blaize, rational thought took over, warning her not to get too close.

"Mexican Vanilla happens to be my favorite, too," she admitted, wishing they didn't have so much in common. It would be easier to walk away if she didn't like him so much.

The rest of the short drive to Amy's was spent in silence. They needed to recalibrate and come up with a plan of attack for the bars. They had time. Ten o'clock was early for the bar scene.

Now that they had a picture of Stephanie, they could ask questions. If she was a regular, a good bartender would know it.

After getting ice cream that Blaize had insisted on paying for, they found a spot at one of the outdoor picnic tables and sat down. He took the seat across from her and leaned in. It was next to impossible not to feel like they were on some kind of date, especially since he paid.

Carys pushed those thoughts aside, tried not to focus on those gorgeous full lips of his—and more importantly, what they could do to her!—and forced a calm over her that she didn't feel.

Fake it till you make it was the worst advice she'd ever heard. It ranked right up there with saying things to yourself in a mirror that you didn't believe. Somewhere deep in the back of your mind, you would know that you were faking it. Except when it came to smiling. Someone had once told her to smile, even when she was in a bad mood, and that worked miracles.

She'd faked being happy to make her father worry less

for too much of her life. It didn't work on him, either. Maybe Blaize was onto something about Rue recording the world around her deep in the back of her mind.

"Are you okay?" Blaize's voice brought her attention back.

"Yes," she said, faking it. Too bad it didn't work like the smile. They had three bars to visit. "Where do you want to go first?"

Chapter Thirteen

"Peggie Hayes is the closest. We should start there first." Being back in Austin brought back a flood of memories. He'd lived here with Lynn, stayed a couple of weeks after she died. Then he moved out closer to his job, where he oversaw the making of custom saddles. There were benefits to growing up on a small cattle ranch. He knew horses and everything that went along with riding or taking care of them. During the summers he gave riding instructions on the weekends at various campsites to bring in extra money.

Money might not make you happy, but lack of it sure as hell didn't help. Medication was expensive, so were doctor bills. Insurance only covered a portion of the costs.

After marrying Lynn, Blaize had drifted away from the handful of friends he'd made over the years. A few of them married and started families. When she got sick, he isolated himself from everyone but her. Work had to be scheduled around doctor appointments. His world shrank. Despite all the hardships during his marriage, he'd loved his wife. It might not have been the same as the stirring he felt from deep within when he was with Carys, but it was love.

"You got quiet," Carys said as they returned to the Jeep.

"Being back here…let's say being here is loaded and

leave it at that." He'd talked enough earlier to become a talk show host.

"Quiet's good."

Neither said much between Amy's and Peggie Hayes. Being in each other's company didn't require words. They sat in comfortable silence, not needing to fill the space.

Peggie Hayes Bar was as funky as it sounded. The walls were covered in graffiti, inside and out. The place was small, the bar big. A dance floor the size of a postage stamp took up the back corner of the room with a jukebox. There was no sawdust on the floor, but country music was as common as mainstream and commercial. Tables had games on them, like trivia, meant for group play.

He parked and then circled around to open her door. They both knew she was fully capable of opening her own door, but he liked doing little things for her, and she smiled and thanked him in response. Her face lit up and his heart galloped.

"Shall we go inside?" he asked. The music thumped. Though crowds hadn't quite formed yet. This would be a good time to hit up the bartender, before business boomed.

"Let's do this," she said with a look of solidarity.

He reached for her hand at the same time she reached for his. They crashed into each other at first, but then their fingers wound through each other's as they fell into step, walking side by side.

Inside, not much had changed. Eleven o'clock was still on the early end for Austin nightlife. He recognized the bartender and saw it as a good sign.

"What can I get you?" the bartender asked, tossing a pair of customized drink coasters onto the bar in front of them. They landed almost perfectly next to each other.

There were half a dozen folks huddled at the opposite

end of the bar. A couple of the tables were full. And there were a few stragglers who'd sidled up to the bar. It was a manageable crowd for one bartender and a barback. The bartender resembled a blond Tom Cruise with a similar height and build. His resemblance to the famous actor was the reason Blaize remembered him.

"Can I ask a question while I decide?" Carys jumped right in.

"Shoot." The bartender stepped a little closer and leaned in as Carys pulled out her phone.

"Any chance you recognize her?" She tilted the screen so he could see.

He backed away and put his hands in the air, palms out. His gaze bounced from Carys to Blaize and back. "I don't want anything to do with whatever you two are up to."

Based on his reaction, Blaize suspected the bartender thought this was an affair situation.

"It's not what you think," he said.

"Look, if you're not here for a drink, then you don't need me."

"I'll take a glass of merlot."

Blaize almost smirked as he thought back to the hand towel. Of course she would take merlot. He made a mental note to buy a bottle for her to celebrate when this was all over and Rue was in good hands.

"Coming right up," Blond Tom Cruise said.

He returned a few moments later with a clean glass and a bottle of wine.

"We're trying to find information about her to locate her next of kin," Blaize said.

"Are you cops?"

"Nothing like that," Blaize said. "Carys works for CPS and wants to reunite Stephanie—that's her name—with her daughter, if we can find her or her family." He searched for a flicker of recognition when he mentioned the name.

No such luck.

"Okay, show me the picture again."

Carys did.

He studied it for a long moment. "I'm sorry, guys. I've never seen this woman before in my life. Even without all the makeup, I don't know who she could be."

Blaize pulled out a twenty and set it on the bar as he stood up. "Thanks. We appreciate your time."

"No problem," Blond Tom Cruise said. "Wish I could be more of a help."

After stepping outside, Carys asked, "Do you think he was lying?"

"No," Blaize confirmed. "I watched for his reactions when I said her name and you showed him the picture. He was drawing a blank, unless he's the best poker player in Texas, in which case he could make a lot more money on the circuit than slinging drinks."

It was a dead end.

"Onto Chord Street," he said.

"All right, then." She reached for his hand, and he linked their fingers as they walked back to the Jeep.

Within a few minutes, they were on the road, navigating through the always rush-hour-like traffic Austin was infamous for. A ten-minute drive in most places could take thirty-five or longer in Texas's capital. Bumper-to-bumper, horns honking, Austin had a rhythm of its own. Still weird. Just more crowded.

The drive took twenty-five minutes. Finding parking took another fifteen. It was nearing midnight by the time they walked into Chord Street Bar.

Two working bartenders manned the clients sitting at the

bar. One was dedicated to the waitstaff, who were already blowing and going. Chord Street was livelier. It was larger with a crush of people standing around bar-height tabletops with no stools. The bar was the center of the establishment.

"Do you want me to send you the picture of Stephanie so we can divide and conquer?" Carys asked after taking in the scene.

"Sounds reasonable."

She let go of his hand and sent the pic. He went left. She went right.

He didn't recognize the bartenders, but this place was larger and there could have been turnover in the last year. A smaller place like Peggie Hayes might have had a better chance of keeping their bartending staff since it had a more family-owned feel.

This was a better place to get lost, blend in, and not be remembered.

Stephanie could have been an employee or a patron. Her name might not even be Stephanie. If she committed to the name change, it made sense that she might've kept at least the first letter of her name for when she signed papers. It wouldn't surprise him if her name was Stephanie or Sarah or in that ballpark.

He moved across the bar from the bartender. She perked up.

"What can I get you?" she asked. She had purple streaks in her hair and tattooed arm sleeves. A nose piercing topped off her look. She might not've been his type or able to hold a candle to Carys, but the look worked for her.

"I'm looking for someone," he said.

She laughed. "Look around, handsome. I'm sure you'll find plenty of 'someones,' based on the looks you're getting."

He wasn't paying attention. "I'm hoping you can help me."

"Okay-y-y-y," she said, moving closer and leaning across the bar. "What can I do for you?"

Someone tried to flag her down from four seats away.

"Be right with you," she said without turning her head.

He pulled up the pic and showed her the screen.

She stared at it for a long moment like she was trying to look beyond the heavy makeup. Her barback walked up and glanced at the screen as he made his way to restock ice, but Blaize was more focused on gauging the bartender's reaction.

"I'm sorry," she finally said. She threw her hands into the air. "I got nothing."

And then she was gone.

Blaize had lost visual on Carys. Panic nailed him as fast as a sucker punch. He pushed off the bar to standing and turned away.

"Excuse me, sir," came an unfamiliar voice.

THE ROOM WAS wall-to-wall people, all looking to have a good time. Carys was completely out of her element here. Having been overprotected as a child caused you to go one of two paths: hog wild or afraid of every new experience. She had fallen into the second category. That fear was probably the reason she couldn't shake the feeling someone had been inside her home. This was a good time to remind herself that fear was irrational. Having a healthy dose was good. It kept you alive. Too much and it paralyzed you. Stopped you from really living or embracing anything unfamiliar.

She'd been out of her father's home for more than six years now, but you didn't easily shake off the ideals that had been ingrained in you.

A slow exhale helped as she navigated her way through the growing crush of people toward the bar.

This side had a male bartender. She squeezed in between two ladies who had their backs to each other and caught his attention. Her phone was already in hand, so she went for it.

"Do you know this person?" she asked.

He barely glanced at the screen. "Nope. What can I get for you?"

"Are you sure about that?"

"A little busy here," he said. "Do you want a drink or not?"

She gave a small headshake and frowned, unable to shake the feeling of eyes on her from somewhere else in the room. Was she being paranoid?

The busy bartender stared at her for a long moment, issued a grunt, and said, "Hold up. Let me take a closer look."

Again, she held out the phone. He studied the pic this time.

"Still no," he said.

"Thank you for your time," she said.

"No problem. Have you been in here before?"

The question caught her off guard considering how rude he'd been a few moments ago.

"No," she said. "Why?"

"Never mind," he said. "I would have remembered you."

Was that a come-on? Because seriously? *Maybe try being less rude when someone first approaches.*

He was five foot ten, maybe eleven. He had sandy-blond hair and gray eyes with a slightly pointed nose—not bad looking by most standards. She was spoiled by Blaize. Now her standards were ridiculously high. Good looks alone didn't do the trick for her. There had to be substance underneath, holding it up. Worse yet, Blaize had that in spades.

Again, he'd raised the standard so high that it would be next to impossible for anyone else to measure up to his looks, him as a person, and certainly the kiss they'd shared. A kiss her body craved to repeat.

Not an option, Carys.

"Thanks for checking out the pic," she said, turning to leave.

"If I'd said that I knew her, would you have stuck around a little longer?"

Gross.

The line didn't deserve a comeback.

When she turned all the way, she practically slammed into Blaize's chest.

"There you are, babe," he said before planting a bone-melting kiss onto her lips, imprinting on her, marking her as his. When he pulled back, he searched her gaze and said, "I was beginning to think I lost you."

A huff sound came from behind the bar.

Carys took Blaize's hand and walked out.

Once outside, he said, "I'm sorry about what I did in there. I thought it was the fastest way to stop him from pestering you." Was there a hint of possessiveness in his tone? Or was she hearing what she wanted to hear instead of what was there?

"Thank you," she said. "The bad part is that he had no idea who Stephanie was, so I didn't make any progress. How did you do?"

He didn't answer right away as they walked through the maze of people on the sidewalk beginning to line up for the bar scene. This was a popular street with several bars and taco joints running along it.

When they reached the Jeep, he turned toward her, glanced around, and said, "The barback asked me to come back closer to closing. Said he would be able to slip me a note."

Carys didn't like it. They could be walking into some kind of ambush.

Or was that old fear creeping in again?

Chapter Fourteen

"Do you want to take a walk or wait here?" They'd been sitting on the ride over, and Blaize wanted to stretch his sore legs.

"I'd like to move," Carys said.

He locked up the Jeep, and they headed east on Chord. Austin was the equivalent of an ant farm of students. They were everywhere, which kept the area safer since there was so much foot traffic. Unhoused folks stayed to themselves, not harassing anyone. It was an easy place to take a walk anytime night or day.

They must have walked, hand in hand, for an hour before stopping for a late-night snack. Blaize bit back a yawn.

"You didn't get much sleep last night," she said. "You must be exhausted."

"All I need is a power nap."

"We can head back to the Jeep after we eat these tacos. I can entertain myself and keep watch while you close your eyes." She checked the time on her phone. "We still have a couple of hours before closing."

He bit back another yawn. "That might not be a bad idea."

Booking a room north of Austin in Round Rock seemed like a bad idea now. He'd intended to keep them north so they could get out of traffic easily tomorrow morning. Being back in Maverick Pass these past days reminded him just how much he loved space. Not much could beat looking up at a Texas sky at night. The expansiveness. The sheer number of stars that he never got to see when he lived in the city thanks to light pollution.

With Cormac gone, he also found a sense of peace at the ranch. Blaize hadn't been expecting to feel anything, especially not like he was right where he belonged. Raiden and Phoenix didn't think the same way. Could he propose a plan to buy them out? Would the bank even give him a loan on the place?

Or could he get his siblings to bet on him? Give them a share if they didn't force him to sell, then pay dividends once he got the place up and profitable? He tucked the idea away for later, hoping for no more unexpected twists in the meantime. Talk about surprises—Kit trying to force the sale had shocked the hell out of him. Had to be her pride talking or a misguided sense of loyalty to her grandsons. Every one of them would have to give up a career in order to move back to the ranch. Blaize's mind was made up. He could start his own business doing what he loved, making custom saddles. He hadn't talked to Phoenix, but according to Raiden their minds were made up, too. Would they listen to Kit?

It dawned on him that she'd called Raiden after learning about Lynn. It would be just like Kit to think of herself as an unfair burden.

Blaize wanted to do this for her. Kit was different from Lynn. Kit appreciated everything he did for her. She always had his best interest at heart. Lynn had become bitter. She'd been frustrated with how her life turned out, which he understood. He'd been a soft pillow for her to throw punches at. He was strong—physically, mentally, and emotionally. He could take it.

"Are you going to eat that?" Carys asked, staring at his untouched taco.

"Do you want it?"

"No. I could always order my own. I thought you were hungry, and you only ate one taco. I know you can eat more than that, so I'm wondering if you're too tired."

He picked up the taco and took a bite. "Torchy's or Velvet?"

"Velvet. Obviously for their chicken tikka tacos."

He laughed. The great Austin debate over the homegrown favorite, Torchy's, versus the Dallas-originated Velvet had a clear winner. They were in agreement, and it was clear that there was no contest in either of their minds.

"Agreed."

"This fried egg on top might be messy, but it's chef's kiss," she said with a smile.

After polishing off the last of his taco, he washed his hands and headed back to the Jeep. All he needed was twenty minutes of shut-eye to grab his second wind. With the activity on the street, he figured they could get away with sitting in the Jeep out in the open without causing any type of disturbance.

Once seated, he leaned his chair back. Carys followed suit, turning onto her left side, facing him, while she studied her cell.

Blaize closed his eyes. A minute later, he drifted off.

TAP. TAP. TAP.

Blaize sat bolt upright. His leg came up, jamming his thigh on the steering wheel. Carys gasped.

A cop stood at the driver's side window, face almost pressing against the glass as he peered inside the Jeep.

Slowly, Blaize lifted his hands and placed them on the wheel in the ten-and-two position so the officer could see them.

"Roll down your window, sir." The cop was squatty, with a ruddy complexion and a serious expression.

With careful movements, Blaize rolled down his manual-crank window.

"I didn't even see him come up," Carys whispered.

A bright light nearly blinded Blaize. He squinted. The officer ran a flashlight over the interior of the Jeep, no doubt checking for weapons or a reason to arrest them like open containers or visible drugs.

"How can I help you, Officer?"

The man's nameplate read *Officer Marcum*.

"You can start by telling me what you're doing here," Officer Marcum said. His gaze shifted to Carys.

"I'm sorry, sir. This is my fault," she said, taking the lead. She reached over to touch Blaize's arm. "My fiancé didn't get much sleep last night after me being in the hospital, so I asked him if we could stop off and rest before making the drive back to Dallas."

Blaize had no idea where any of this was coming from, but he wasn't about to argue.

Marcum's gaze shifted from Carys to him. "Are you aware that it's not advisable to sleep in a parking lot?"

"Yes, sir. I am now." He rubbed his eyes.

Carys patted her stomach. "We had a scare. I started spotting, and we thought…" Her chin quivered. "That maybe we were about to lose this little bean."

Damn. She was good at this.

"Sorry to hear that, ma'am." Marcum's intensity scaled down a few notches.

"Is there a convenient place to grab coffee for my fiancé nearby before we head out?" she asked. She played the role to perfection. Blaize needed to ask if she had any acting in her background.

"Convenience store is on the corner," he said. "Go straight this way."

"Will do. Thanks."

Officer Marcum turned to Blaize. "License and insurance, please. Before you head out."

"My insurance is on my phone. Hold on." He grabbed his cell and then located the card before showing the officer the screen. When Marcum nodded, Blaize fished out his wallet and then produced his license.

The cop took it and examined it. He excused himself and walked back to his vehicle. He was punching in the information on a laptop that looked like it was attached to the dashboard on a moveable tray. He must have been satisfied with what he found because he strolled over and handed the ID back. "Y'all be safe on the road."

"Will do." Carys beamed. "Thank you, Officer."

Marcum gave a small salute before disappearing around the back of the Jeep and back to his own vehicle. Blaize turned on the engine after rolling up his window.

"What should we do?" she asked.

"Circle the block a few times. Park farther from the bar. He was probably expecting one or both of us to be drunk and unable to drive." He navigated out of the parking lot and onto the road, moving in the direction of the convenience store the officer had mentioned to make it look good. The cop sat in his vehicle, typing away on the laptop as they drove off.

Avoiding a second encounter with the same officer would be ideal. There were enough people around they should be able to blend in.

"You don't think we're being set up, do you?" Carys asked as he turned right at the end of the street. "By the barback?"

"We should come up with a plan, just in case."

"You're right," she said.

"How long was I asleep?" He glanced at the time, muttered a curse. Too long. They only had twenty minutes until the meetup. "We'll have to figure out a parking spot fast and a plan even faster." Parking was a joke in downtown Austin. Try parking illegally and you could end up towed. Not having transportation would be complicated, especially if this was a setup.

"Tell me again what happened," she said. After the cop encounter, he realized how good she was at thinking under pressure. "We can start there."

"A young guy, early twenties, walked past while I was showing Stephanie's picture to the female bartender. I noticed him because he seemed interested. He came around the bar and caught my arm when I walked toward your side. Said he couldn't talk right now but that I should meet him closer to closing time."

"I don't like this," she said.

"He wants me to meet. He's not a big guy. If it's just him, I'm not worried."

"If he has information about Stephanie, why ask you to come back? Why not tell you what he knows right then?"

"Those are good questions," he said, banking a left. "I don't have answers. All I have is someone who wants to tell me something about the person in the picture. With two of us, we can figure out a failsafe if the guy is up to something."

"This whole meetup makes me nervous." Carys twisted her fingers together in her lap. "There are too many what-ifs and no proof this person has useful information."

"At least we know there are a lot of cops around if this thing goes south."

Carys shook her head. "Maybe this isn't such a good idea."

"It's all we have."

"We still have one bar left," she said.

"Which isn't as good of a lead."

"We don't know that," she said. "All we know for certain is that someone asked to meet after work. How far away from the picture was he?"

"A foot behind the bartender." If that much.

"And you said he walked past. As in, he kept going."

"That's correct."

"Which means he barely got a glance at the picture," she said.

"I wouldn't say that." Blaize had a good feeling about the guy. "What reason could he have for speaking up? Why not just let me walk out the door? The bartender didn't know anything. Why raise suspicion?"

"THAT'S A GOOD POINT." *Breathe.* They might've been getting close to a breakthrough. "I'm freaking out over your safety." And the general feeling of not being able to control the situation. Turned out being overly protected as a kid could cause you to need to control everything.

"I'll be careful." Blaize's reassurance sent a wave of calm washing over her and through her. "Believe it or not, I'm pretty good at keeping myself alive. There've been plenty of times that I've been out on the land, staring down wild hogs capable of killing me on the spot and had to come up with an escape plan. I've faced down poachers and survived. I'll take any and every threat seriously, but I didn't get that kind of vibe from this guy. He looked concerned and maybe a little scared to speak to me. Does any of this help ease your concerns?"

He pulled into a newly available street-side parking spot. That was lucky.

"It does," she said before reaching out to touch his arm. The contact was electric, as she was beginning to expect whenever they touched. It was also tender enough to cause her breath to catch in her throat and her stomach to freefall like she'd just base jumped. "A surprising amount actually."

"Good." He leaned over. "Because I'll be careful and you'll be watching my back. We have no reason to believe the barback saw us together in that crowd."

It had been shoulder-to-shoulder in the room.

"Why do you think he might be scared?" she asked. "If you had to guess."

"Could be for a lot of reasons." If he leaned any closer, they would be within kissing range. "Like he knows why she ended up in a fiery car crash."

"As far as we know, it was a lone vehicle accident." She hadn't considered this could be a murder investigation. So far, she assumed Stephanie was hiding both herself and her child from a potentially abusive relationship.

Would the father of her child have murdered her?

"Without a murder investigation, the sheriff won't look into her text messages," she said after taking a moment to think. A thought struck. "I've been going back and forth on whether she's alive or gone but that might be wishful thinking for Rue's sake. Do you think there's a possibility Stephanie Cross is alive?"

"No," Blaize said. "Although I learned a long time ago to never say *never*."

Carys let the thought sit before trying to unpack it.

All they had right now was very little information and a whole mess of speculation. Going down a trail of what-ifs with this little to go on could be counterproductive and end up getting them lost.

They needed to stick to what they knew was fact, despite how much her brain wanted to fill in the holes. She also needed to tread lightly on this case and not leave a digital or paperwork trail that could come back to bite her in the backside.

Besides, there were too many questions in this case.

With this barback, they might get answers.

Chapter Fifteen

Blaize sat on a step two doors down from the bar in the back alley. The barback would have to empty the trash as part of his closing duties. This spot would give Blaize an advantage. He could clearly see the door from this vantage point. From farther down the alley, Carys could keep watch over him. She had a tire iron from his Jeep to use as a weapon or, better yet, figure out how to give to him if something went south.

The door opened. He tried not to move a muscle or breathe. The barback stepped outside with a full trash bag, as anticipated. He kicked a bucket over to stop the door from closing. It must've locked automatically.

Blaize scanned the area in search of any suspicious movement. The barback hadn't explicitly asked Blaize to meet outside. In fact, he probably expected a visit in the bar before closing like he'd requested. A thin crowd meant the possibility of eyes on them, exposing the barback for possible retribution. The guy came across like he was sticking his neck out. Blaize wanted to honor it.

"Pssst," he hissed in an attempt to get the guy's attention without freaking him out.

"Hey, Thomas." The male bartender stepped outside and lit a smoke. "Why didn't you stock the glasses under the bar like I told you to? Now it'll take even more time to close out, and I can't leave here until everything is stocked."

Thomas. Blaize had a first name to work with now.

Thomas's gaze flicked over toward the spot where Blaize was sitting. Did the guy just give them away?

"We were slammed all night," Thomas said, pushing back. "Last I checked, I only have two hands and you kept me hopping all night. Or don't you remember?"

Thomas was skinny and in need of a haircut. He had blond hair and light eyes, looked to be a freshman in college or maybe a sophomore at most.

"Excuses," the bartender said, leaning his back against the bricks. He brought his foot up, sole flat against the wall. "Just because you're Angel's nephew doesn't mean you can't get fired."

"Go ahead, then," Thomas said, unfazed. "Tell my uncle that I'm doing a bad job and you want me gone. See how that works out for you while you're out here smoking instead of pitching in. You know, we'll lock up a hell of a lot faster if you put out that cigarette and get back to work."

The bartender flinched like he was about to throw a punch.

"Go ahead and do it," Thomas teased. "Or get out of my way so I can toss the trash into the dumpster, dude."

Blaize liked the kid's spunk. He took note of the fact that the guy's uncle was important to the bar. Manager? Owner?

A squad car turned down the alley.

If the same cop from a little while ago was behind the wheel, Blaize was busted. How much trouble could he get into for being caught lying to an officer? He needed to signal Carys to get out of there. She was positioned down the alley far enough to slip into the groups of folks walking around or standing in line at one of the nearby taco food trucks lining the street.

Could he slip away unseen? Join her?

A quick glance revealed her coming toward him with her back against the wall. *No, no, no.*

From the corner of his eye, he caught the bartender dropping the cigarette butt before crushing it underneath his shoe. He slipped inside and, like the jerk he was proving to be, tapped the bucket away, causing the door to close and lock.

"What are you doing?" he whispered to Carys as she approached. "You had a chance to escape." There was a slim possibility the officer—if it was him—wouldn't have recognized Blaize without her. With her, it was almost a given.

Instead of responding, she fisted his shirt and tugged him up to standing. Then she pressed up to her tiptoes, turned them so that her back was against the wall, and pulled him toward her until their mouths fused.

The cop car crept down the alley, coming toward them, but for a split second, Blaize lost all sense of time and place. The second her lips met his, fireworks exploded in his chest, the world tilted on its axis, and he felt like he was right where he was supposed to be.

With great effort, Blaize forced his attention back to the alley and out of the blissful fog of need.

He heard Thomas swearing along with the sounds of the oversized trash bag being forced into an already-full dumpster.

Next came the hum of the vehicle's engine. It stopped. A window rolled down.

"You can't stay here. Move on." The officer's unfamiliar voice caused Blaize to exhale.

"Sorry," he said, moving to take Carys by the hand and heading toward Thomas without making eye contact.

The squad car sat idle. The officer was likely assessing whether he believed they were sober. They must have passed because the engine hummed and rocks crunched underneath the tires.

Thomas cursed as he tried the door.

"Hey," Blaize said as they approached, hand in hand.

Thomas whirled around, his hands fisted. Right. He probably couldn't make out the sound of Blaize's voice over the loud noises in the bar earlier where voices fought to be heard over the music.

"It's me," Blaize said.

Thomas sighed relief. "You scared the sh—" His gaze bounced from Blaize to Carys and back. "Anyway, I wasn't sure if you would show."

"I'm here. What did you want to tell me?"

The kid looked around, eyes wild, like he half expected someone to jump out from behind a dumpster. "I could get into a lot of trouble for this." He caught Blaize's gaze. "Like, serious trouble."

"I appreciate you trusting me, Thomas. But you haven't said anything yet. Do you want to see the pic again?"

"No," Thomas said, looking taken aback with the fact Blaize said his name. "I never liked how my uncle treated her, you know?"

"Sure." Blaize had no idea.

Thomas hesitated.

"Before long, another cop is going to drive down the alley or someone is going to open that door to see what's taking you so long to close up," Blaize said. "You'll save us all a lot of angst if you'll spit it out." All kinds of scenarios came to mind, none he liked. Blaize needed to hear the truth before his imagination got the best of him.

"She worked here about a year ago," Thomas said. "Nice lady. I overheard her arguing with my uncle."

He glanced around like the man might jump out and say, *Boo!* He sucked in a breath before continuing. "Two days later, she disappeared, and I haven't seen her since."

"Did you hear what they were saying?" Carys jumped in.

"No, but my uncle isn't exactly… He runs this place on the up and up, but this isn't his only business. People come in and out of here. And it's not good."

"Got it," Blaize said. The timing of her going missing matched with her pregnancy. Was Angel the baby's father?

"What's her name? The woman in the picture?" Carys asked.

"Sharon Clark," Thomas said. "Her roommate got her the job. I sneaked into my uncle's office after you left." He pulled a slip of paper out of his apron pocket and handed it to Blaize. "It's their address. Or, at least, it was. Haley quit about a month after Sharon."

A random person shouted, and the sound echoed. It was enough to spook Thomas. "I've gotta go. I just hope you find her and that she's okay."

"Why are you helping us?" Carys asked.

"Because she was nice to me and doesn't deserve to have anything bad happen to her," Thomas said. He took off running around the line of buildings. "Keep me out of it."

The back door to the bar creaked before it opened. The noise gave them enough time to dive behind the dumpster and out of view.

"Thomas. Where the hell did you go?" The bartender's voice was familiar. He cursed and then shut the door. The lock clicked.

Blaize tucked the paper into his front jeans pocket, reached for Carys's hand, and then sprinted in the opposite direction of Thomas.

CARYS'S THIGHS BURNED and her side cramped. Blaize was a faster runner. She strained to keep up as he practically dragged her along, urging her to keep pace with every forward step.

They came to a hard stop at the Jeep. She bent forward, clutched her side, and gasped for air.

"Are you okay?" he asked, moving beside her and placing his hand on the small of her back.

"I will be," she managed to say through breaths. Standing up straight, she motioned toward his pocket.

He nodded before pulling the piece of paper out of his pocket. Why wasn't he breathing hard? To say the man was in good shape was a lot like saying butter melted on warm toast.

"Here's the address." He showed it to her.

Carys pulled out her phone and mapped the location. "MLK Boulevard. I know the area."

"I do, too," he said.

"We should get some rest," he said. "Investigating the house now will cast suspicion that we can't afford."

"The cop ran your license." That was tricky. "We'll have to be even more careful moving forward now that there's a record of us being here."

"That was bad luck."

A shower and sleep sounded like heaven right now. Carys checked the location of the hotel. "We're not far."

Blaize walked her to the passenger side and then opened the door. "For what it's worth, you're the bravest person I know."

She highly doubted that. Didn't the man have a mirror? Talk about bravery. She couldn't imagine holding your loved one's hand as they slowly slipped away from you. "You're pretty amazing yourself."

"I wasn't fishing for a compliment." He hesitated. "I get the sense you're uncomfortable with being told how great you are. And how beautiful you are."

She really blushed now.

"As long as you're around me, I hope you'll get used to hearing it."

Blaize wasn't making it any easier *not* to fall for him. He needed to stop before she asked for another kiss—a kiss that was forbidden. Not to mention they'd agreed kissing would be a bad idea.

"We should get going," she managed to say through a throat suddenly as dry as Texas soil in August. "I need a shower and a bed."

He hesitated, looked like he was about to say something else, then closed her door and walked around the front of the Jeep wearing the sexiest smirk. He shook his head before claiming the driver's seat and didn't say a word to her on the way to the hotel or when they checked in.

The standard room had one bed—king size, a desk, and a comfy-looking chair with a reading lamp positioned behind it. The bed looked more like a cloud and was plenty large enough for the two of them to sleep without touching each other. Blaize could take up two-thirds, and there would still be plenty of room left for her.

"You take the shower first," he said.

"Are you sure?"

"Go ahead. Take your time."

Carys carried her overnight bag into the bathroom. The bag made her think of home. The feeling someone had been inside her house returned as she set it down on the counter, stripped, and then eased into the shower.

What was up with the feeling and why did she feel off?

Carys almost laughed out loud. The answer came quickly. Everything. Rue turned her life upside down in a heartbeat.

No regrets.

She'd made a promise to herself a long time ago when she first moved away from her father and to college. Whatever mistakes she made from then on belonged to her and no one else. She would no longer have her father to blame if life wasn't going the way she'd hoped it would. She would no longer have a failsafe to offer a soft landing. And she would no longer have an excuse to be unhappy.

From then on, she'd decided, her mistakes were just going to be part of the tapestry of her life. More importantly, they would be *hers*. And she was okay with that.

Which meant no regrets.

Did the same apply about Blaize? Or could she ask him for a kiss tonight after all?

Chapter Sixteen

Blaize didn't need the naked image of Carys in the shower with beads of water rolling down her silky skin stamped in his thoughts. It had been a long day. They needed rest. That was probably the reason his emotions took the wheel, defied logic, and refused to stop thinking about her.

The best way to stop thinking about someone was with a good workout. His muscles were stiff from all the sitting on the drive to Austin. Then there'd been driving around Austin. They'd walked a little and run a bit—not nearly enough movement to fulfill his body's needs.

The water cut off. He shouldered his backpack.

When the bathroom door opened and Carys walked out, he realized how unprepared he was to see her in pajama shorts and a soft cotton T-shirt. The thin material hinted at revealing her full breasts.

Blood flew south as he stood up, walked past, and then exhaled when he closed the bathroom door behind him. A workout could wait. A shower could ease some of the muscle tension. It wasn't taking all his considerable willpower to force his body not to act on its own accord.

Would she welcome his touch? His kiss?

Rather than fall down that rabbit hole, he took a cold shower and threw on a pair of pajama pants. Normally, he wore boxers to bed. He'd packed the lounge pants for her sake.

Blaize cut off the light as he opened the door and realized he was in complete darkness. It was fine. He'd memorized the layout and could navigate getting to bed all right without tripping over anything as long as he kept one hand on the wall.

His phone sat on the desk. He made his way over without bumping a shin—a miracle. Carys's soft, steady breathing said she was already asleep. She probably conked out the second her head hit the pillow.

After dimming his screen, he slipped underneath the covers. The temptation to pull her into his arms was a physical ache.

He closed his eyes and refocused. Tires. Those were the least sexy things he could think about. He needed to get new tires on his Jeep in the near future.

As though sensing his mental battle, Carys rolled over and settled into the crook of his arm. She slung her leg over his. He was thankful for the thin layers of material preventing skin from touching bare skin. That would be his undoing.

Eventually, he drifted off.

THE SUN PEEKED through the small slit in the curtains Blaize had kept open. Blackout curtains threw him off too much. He didn't know when to open his eyes if they were closed all the way. It was disorienting. He needed the sun as much as he needed the expansive Texas sky.

Carys's warm limbs entwined with his. Her hair splayed across the pillow. She smelled like a field of wildflowers.

Caffeine. Blaize needed to untangle himself or risk waking her, and he sure as hell couldn't stay there while his fingers burned to touch every curve of that beautiful body.

With effort, he managed to slide away and out from underneath the covers. A glance at his phone said it was half past nine in the morning. He couldn't remember the last time he'd slept this late no matter what time he went to bed.

The sun was bright. He moved quietly through the room, made coffee, and washed up. After a cup, he could figure out what to do about food. There was probably a power bar in his backpack tucked in the front pocket. He usually kept that or a small bag of trail mix for easy access to keep from starving.

After sitting down to nurse his coffee, he checked the address again. He looked it up using the map feature on his phone. The house was listed on a popular real estate site five years ago. The pictures were still up. The two-bedroom light yellow house had a one-vehicle carport and black metal bars on the windows. Electric cables ran on the street out front. The yard was small, not giving much separation from the busy street. A small tree blocked much of the house from view.

Inside, the front door led straight into the living room. The kitchen was eat-in. Both bedrooms were in the back of the house. The place was surrounded by low trees that could offer some coverage as they approached.

If the occupants had a dog, they would be busted walking up. Could he and Carys come up with a reason for being there? Knock on the front door? Put on some type of maintenance jumper?

Where would they get one? It wasn't like they sold uniforms at the local big-box store.

Then again, he wouldn't know. It wasn't like he spent a

lot of time in those places. He got in and out as fast as possible on the occasion he needed to go inside one.

Back to the phone screen, he studied the layout of the home. He "walked" the neighborhood as best as he could to get the lay of the land. Once on the ground, they needed to appear they knew what they were doing or risk drawing attention. Could they walk down the street holding hands? Pretend to be a couple like they had last night? The move was starting to feel a little too natural with Carys, like they had a rhythm and had been together in another lifetime. Or something like that.

Hell, he didn't normally go full-on romantic. She had a way of bringing out a different side to him. Or maybe he was just trying to rationalize an attraction that was never meant to be understood.

It had been so long since he'd been on a date, would he even know what one looked like now? Not to mention the fact Carys was almost ten years younger than him. Were they too far apart in age? Did they want different things at this point in their lives?

Funny. He didn't want anything except to save the ranch and keep Kit where she belonged. Forty-eight hours made a helluva difference in life. With Lynn, he was reminded that life could change on a dime. With Carys, he saw that as a good thing.

"What time is it?" Carys asked, sitting up and gently rubbing her eyes.

He glanced at the clock. "Ten fifteen."

"I overslept," she said, pushing the covers off and throwing long legs over the side. He couldn't help but remember how good it felt when she'd entwined them with his.

"No, it's fine."

"Are you sure? You must be starving by now," she said

as she stretched. He forced his gaze away from the way the cotton pressed against her breasts.

"I'm good. I haven't been awake for very long. This is my first cup of coffee, and I'm about to make my second. Would you like one, or do you need food first?"

"What do you think about ordering room service?"

"We might be too late for breakfast."

"A hamburger and fries sound amazing to me right now," she said, a sleepy smile tugging at the corners of her mouth. Damned if the knot didn't tighten in his chest.

He picked up the menu. "Consider it done."

"What can I do to help?"

"Let me spoil you for a change," he said, and he meant every word. "I like doing things for you that make your life easier."

Was it a mistake to admit that to her?

CARYS SMILED ON her way to the bathroom. "I'm not going to tell you no."

As she brushed her teeth, she heard Blaize on the phone ordering from the lunch menu. Her systems were turned upside down. Her body didn't know day from night at this point. It wanted protein. Besides, she didn't know when she'd get a chance to eat again. Her schedule was all over the place until this case resolved.

Speaking of days of the week, she thought for a moment and realized it was already Sunday. How could she go into the office on Monday if she still had Rue in her custody? *That's tomorrow-Carys's problem.* Besides, she had plenty to focus on today.

Practically, they could investigate the house and get back to the ranch by dinner. They had a new name to work with—Sharon Clark.

She thought about the name Stephanie Cross…a potential fake name. *Were you hiding from this Angel person? What was he to you? An ex-boyfriend?*

Thomas didn't explain what he meant about not liking how his uncle treated her. And now they knew she used to work at the bar. This was like being expected to put together a five-hundred-piece puzzle with a couple of pieces and none of the rest.

These things take time.

Did she have any?

Carys dressed in yoga pants, a sports bra, and a tank top. She pulled her hair off her face into a ponytail. Push come to shove, she could pass for someone being out on a jog. Being a college town, Austin was a lively place, especially the downtown area. Joggers could be seen throughout the day, seven days a week. She should fit right in.

A knock on the door told her she'd been in the bathroom way longer than expected or that room service in this hotel was speedy.

She waited until Blaize answered, then came out of the bathroom once the server was gone since the doors would clash otherwise.

"Food's here," Blaize said in that oh-so-sexy deep timbre of his. That man could read the contents of a cereal box and make women want to start peeling off their clothes.

She laughed.

"What's that about?" He studied her, perplexed.

No way was she sharing that little tidbit.

"Nothing," she said. "This food smells amazing."

"You're probably starving, which helps." He finished setting up the makeshift table and chairs. He directed her to sit in the office-like chair while he took the bed.

She picked up the metal lid and was hit with a waft of awesomeness. "Yes to all of this."

He chuckled. "Do you always go full force at life?"

She had a bite of food in her mouth that she almost spit out from laughing. Once she chewed and swallowed, she said, "Since I moved out. I was kept locked up basically my entire childhood. Once I adjusted to college life, I decided to just run at life full-steam-ahead style. I own my mistakes and do my best to learn from them."

"It's a good philosophy," he said.

"I'm so much happier now. Even when I screw up, and believe me, I have royally done so. Knowing my missteps are my own has its own healing energy attached. Being under someone's thumb is the worst kind of existence."

"I can partially relate. It's no life."

"That's why I feel so sorry for Stephanie or Sharon, whatever her name is." She took a sip of the coffee he'd fixed for her. "This happened to me when I was young. Plus, it was my father. He may have broken our relationship, but he does love me. Or did. I haven't talked to him in too long to know where he stands now. It was misguided love—don't get me wrong. It was action born out of loss and sadness and fear. But I never once doubted that he loved me."

Blaize listened. Truly listened. He didn't try to fix things, like guys she'd dated. And because of that, she felt seen.

"Would you ever want to reach out to see if anything has changed between the two of you?" he asked. "No pressure. I'm just curious."

"I've thought about it. A lot of time has passed. More than six years." She took a bite of hamburger and chewed. "I'm not ready yet to handle the disappointment if he didn't change. The last thing I want is to reopen an old wound just to throw salt in it. You know? Does that make sense?"

"Sure, it does. You would want to have a relationship if he has changed and grown over the years, but sometimes not knowing is better than suffering more disappointment."

"That's it exactly. What if he remarried and has another family? What if he rejects me and doesn't have a new family? What if he just doesn't care what happens to me?"

Blaize nodded.

They settled into eating and polishing off his second and her first cup of coffee.

"What will your work do when they find out you didn't take Rue to the orphanage?" he asked as he stacked plates on the rollaway tray.

"That depends."

"On what?"

"What happens between now and Monday morning."

"Then let's make sure you don't lose your job over helping an innocent baby," he said with the kind of finality that made her believe him. "I'll just be a minute while I get dressed."

"I'll scoot the cart into the hallway now that we're finished."

He reached for her hand, stopped her from moving the cart. "Might be safer to leave it inside while we get ready. The less we open and close doors, the better."

"Do you think someone followed us?"

"I'd rather not find out the hard way. I didn't tell Thomas my name, and I paid with cash at the first bar on purpose. Still. Taking a chance doesn't seem like the right play here."

He was right. Of course he was. For a moment, she felt imprisoned again. Beyond her father's tight grip, she'd endured everything from being locked in closets by babysitters to being threatened within an inch of her life if she "ratted" out the ones having sex on her father's bed or drinking to the point of passing out while he had to be away on business.

From a young age, Carys understood the fact that her father's job kept food on the table. He worked long hours balancing the finances so he could pay his workers while keeping a roof over her head. She caught glimpses of him looking run down—and an emotion that looked a whole lot like guilt—but he always put up a strong front when she was in the room. Telling him about the babysitters would have only added to his stress. Besides, she'd learned to keep emergency supplies in the form of a flashlight, book, and a chocolate bar in a couple of the closets just to be safe and stave off boredom.

As much as she shouldn't care about anyone else rubber-stamping her life decisions, her relationship with her father was tricky. The urge to make him proud constantly warred with her need to prove her independence, causing a ton of friction in her high school years.

Families and relationships were complicated. No one knew that better than Blaize.

Shake it off.

Mentally, she had to readjust. This was not the past. She was free to go wherever she wanted to go and do whatever she wanted to do. Her father still lived near Austin as far as she knew.

Carys, of all people, knew what it was like to be trapped by someone hell-bent on controlling her and being surrounded by people who carried out that person's bidding.

Is this how you felt, Sharon?

Chapter Seventeen

A simple spit test was all it would take to prove Blaize wasn't Rue's father. So why couldn't he bring himself to stop by a pharmacy and pick up a test? It was more than Rue's safety he was concerned about.

Taking the test meant closing the door on being the one legally allowed to raise her. Could he see himself as a single father? What about the ranch? Kit? Was there any way possible to fit all the pieces together and be a family?

And what about this Stephanie/Sharon person. His mind was all over the place. One part said she died in the crash and they were awaiting confirmation. Another part said she went into hiding and faked her death. Yet another part wondered if she'd gone into Witness Protection. Or did she simply disappear once she learned about the crash?

Creating a fake identity was possible with computers.

What about Thomas? He seemed like a good person. Could he be trusted? He'd said his uncle was connected to Stephanie/Sharon. How? Why?

Too many questions. Not nearly enough answers.

Blaize should be used to life throwing him twists by this point. Unless he uncovered a hidden tackle box full of cash at the ranch, he wasn't sure how to save it. His brothers were united against him. Kit, of all people, had been the one to convince them to sell.

What was she thinking?

Maybe he should jump at the opportunity to rid himself of the responsibility of the ranch. He couldn't. Taking away Kit's home felt like the worst kind of wrong. He knew in his heart that she didn't want that to happen.

Could he make his brothers see it, too?

Cormac Wilde's death might have brought Blaize back to Maverick Pass, Texas, where Blaize had grown up, but raising a daughter might make him decide to stick around once the dust settled.

Damn that he'd lost touch with his brother and pushed Kit away. Guilt punched him again. If he'd done a better job of staying in touch, he might not have been blindsided by the state of the ranch.

Kit had dropped a bomb on him about his father. He needed to have a sit-down with her to find out what in Cormac's past could possibly excuse his behavior. *Complicated* didn't begin to describe Blaize's emotions since hearing of the man's passing. His brothers must've been in the same boat. They all had a difficult relationship with their father, if *difficult* was the right word.

Digging into Stephanie/Sharon's background could stir up big trouble based on Thomas's reaction. It dawned on Blaize that the car attacker from the other night might have been related to her and not someone from Carys's past.

Speaking of Carys. Blaize hadn't felt an emotional pull this strong since…well…ever. The redheaded beauty challenged every belief he ever held about how deep an attraction could run and how impossible it could be to fight against it. This one was stronger than he dared admit to himself or anyone else. Seeing her hold the child stirred up a whole bunch of feelings that had been dormant. Becoming a father had been put in the *For Other People* category once Lynn closed the door to the possibility. After the terminal diagnosis, any thoughts of changing her mind had to be put on the backburner so he could care for Lynn. She'd been dead set against adoption, too. Said she couldn't see putting a child through her mood swings.

Blaize had had the same concern even though he hadn't owned up to it with her.

Now that being a parent might not just be possible but could be a safety net for a little girl, too, he needed to deal with feelings that had been shoved down so deep he wondered if they could be resurrected.

There was another consideration. If he didn't take the spit test, could Carys let him keep Rue and then walk away like he'd never argued against the idea of her being his biological child?

She might've been one to bend the rules when necessary but that was big.

He was getting ahead of himself. They needed to figure out who this Stephanie/Sharon person really was, and they had a solid lead.

Blaize finished getting dressed and packed up the few clothing and supplies he'd brought, tabling those thoughts for the time being.

"Are you ready to roll?" Blaize asked Carys.

She smiled and raised her eyebrows. "As ready as I'll ever be."

"Let's go," he said, taking the lead after shouldering his backpack.

Once safely in the Jeep, Carys asked, "Should we check on how things are going back home?"

She probably meant home as in Maverick Pass and not

home as in the ranch. He still liked hearing how the word rolled off her tongue so easily and how natural it sounded in conversation.

"I texted earlier, but a phone call would be good." He motioned toward his phone, which he'd placed inside the cupholder. "Do you mind? They won't pick up if you call. Kit is trained not to answer calls from strangers." He chuckled. "It goes against her nature."

"Sounds like Kit." She picked up the phone. The screen came to life. "You don't password protect your cell?"

"No need. I live alone and I work alone." Why did that make him sound so lonely all of a sudden?

Speaking of lonely, he remembered one of the people he'd spent time talking to at Deep Roots Bar. Sierra Jones. She'd walked up to the stool beside him and asked to sit. The fact that she was alone and not with girlfriends didn't raise any big red flags. Deep Roots was the kind of place where folks showed up when they didn't want to be alone and didn't necessarily have to talk to anyone. It was dimly lit inside, a place where conversations were more like a quiet hum.

The first night Sierra had walked up beside him, he barely noticed her. Would she be considered beautiful by most standards? She was tall with long legs. Her long straight dark hair fell between her shoulder blades. She always wore a skirt that hugged her hips and highlighted one of her best features, her legs. She had almond-shaped, catlike green eyes accented with black eyeliner. She smelled of expensive perfume and carried a handbag that he was sure was designer. Yet she had a salt-of-the-earth quality that made her easy to talk to. Or maybe it was the whiskey. Hell, he didn't know.

"No answer," Carys said.

"We'll try again in a few minutes."

"Do you think everything is all right?" she asked.

"I hope so. We'll give it a minute."

Carys set the phone down and stared out the window, looking lost in her own thoughts. As for his, they drifted back to Sierra. She'd been the one to strike up a conversation first. Blaize swore to himself that he wouldn't fall in love again or consider the "marriage and kids" bit. Neither talked about the past. They were two strangers in a bar who slowly started to open up to each other. Or so he thought. Weeks went by and he started looking forward to Tuesday nights at Deep Roots, to seeing Sierra.

He should have looked for the signs, but his guard was down.

Sierra asked him to go to her place for a nightcap. He'd declined.

She didn't show for two weeks. He had no way to reach her to say he hadn't meant to hurt her feelings. She didn't know about Lynn. He talked about work and the fact that he'd been married. That was it. He couldn't bring himself to discuss Lynn's illness or any of the details of their life together. Sierra assumed divorce, and he didn't correct her.

She talked to him about the difficulties of raising her kids essentially alone, a boy and a girl. The twins were nine years old. She talked about carpools and sports, summer camps. She went on about how difficult it was to manage everyone's schedule, including her own. A couple of months passed. They started meeting up twice a week.

This was the early days after Lynn had passed. Sierra said she wasn't looking for a relationship, which worked out great because he didn't have anything left of himself to give.

Then it was three times.

Not exchanging phone numbers should have been his first red flag. He'd be so lost in his own grief that his guard was down. Then he realized he'd slipped up and developed feelings for Sierra.

He convinced himself they weren't strong. Told himself this was a phase and it would pass. The invitation stood, she'd said, to go back to her place any time. He took that as a sign she was developing feelings for him, too.

Blaize didn't do casual sex, not even when he was swimming in grief.

Then he broke their unspoken agreement one night after one too many whiskeys. He opened a vein and said he'd developed feelings for her that were more than bar meetups. Once again, she suggested a hookup.

His thinking wasn't clear. Grief mixed with whiskey didn't do good things to a person's brain or judgment. So, he'd laid his cards out on the table and said he wanted to take her on a dinner date and then another after that. He wanted to see if they had anything in common besides bar stools.

The minute he mentioned that he might be open to a relationship if things went well, Sierra dropped a bombshell on him: She was still married and wouldn't dream of leaving her husband, who traveled a lot, leaving her lonely and with nothing to do to fill the time.

She'd told him that she had an arrangement with her husband that allowed them both "extracurricular" activities but that she would never risk a divorce.

Blaize had been angry at himself more than anything else for falling into the trap of developing real feelings. Plus, he no longer trusted his judgment if he could so easily be lied to.

He'd bought the lies and never once questioned why

she kept insisting on a hookup rather than trying to build something real. Guess he wasn't great at catching red flags while he was drowning in grief.

Was anyone?

"Did you notice the SUV with blacked-out windows following us?" The concern in Carys's voice shocked him back to the present.

He'd been distracted with memories and could have gotten them killed.

Dammit.

A memory came back in a flash. It was hazy. There'd been someone who took the barstool next to him at Deep Root after Sierra left the night of his confession. A blonde. Medium height and build. His memory might be foggy, but she looked familiar.

Could the person have been Stephanie/Sharon?

BLAIZE CHECKED HIS mirrors and frowned. "How long has the SUV been trailing us?"

"Long enough for me to notice, so more than a couple of blocks at this point," Carys said. He'd gone somewhere dark in his mind. She'd seen the wrinkle in his forehead and the way his jaw ticked whenever he was deep in thought.

"I need to get us away from traffic," he said. "If we slow down anymore, they'll be able to get out of their vehicle and walk to us."

Carys had been uncomfortable ever since the phone call that had rolled into voicemail. Maybe a better word was *unsettled.* Something felt off. It was possible Kit was taking a nap along with the baby. Raiden wouldn't answer her phone for her, so it wasn't exactly time to hit the panic button. Still. She was uneasy.

Would Raiden call if something had happened? He should. There was no reason to keep Blaize in the dark.

Her mind had been drifting all over the place until the SUV. Now she studied the sideview mirror, waiting to see if the driver or a passenger made a move. With the sun's glare and the window tint—tint that should've been illegal if it wasn't already—it was impossible to see if there was anyone else in the vehicle other than the driver. The only reason she knew someone sat in the driver's seat was because it made logical sense.

Breathe.

"Slide down in your seat as much as possible in case..."

Carys did as instructed as she finished the sentence in her mind...*they shoot.*

He weaved in and out of traffic like a skilled race-car driver. She did her best not to panic about all the unknowns in this situation.

"Bear with me."

"Okay."

Blaize cut across two lanes of traffic and banked a right with so much speed she could swear they went up on two tires. At the very least, the tires squealed.

"Grab a phone, either one, and look up nearby police substations," he said. "We don't have a reason to call 911. Should that change, you'll have your phone in hand and ready to go."

Carys grabbed his since it was closest. She checked the map feature, half holding her breath as she searched for a substation. He was right, though—a criminal wouldn't likely follow them into the parking lot of a cop station. Officers could be on shift change or drifting in and out of the lot for other reasons.

"You're going to want to take a left at the next light,"

she said to him after risking a glance out the front windshield to verify.

"Hold on," he said.

Carys braced herself as he cut a hard, last-minute left turn. Her stomach churned, a mix of stress, speed, and being tossed around.

The seat belt locked, cutting into her chest.

"What else?" he asked.

She refocused on the screen. "Did I mention that I get seasick?" Trying to focus on the device made her stomach turn even more. She wished she had one of those motion-sickness patches she'd heard about.

"I'm sorry, Carys."

"I know," she said through measured breaths. "Maybe sitting up would help."

He nodded.

She pushed up enough to ease some of the queasiness. "Go straight through this light. We're a little more than two blocks away."

"Got it," he said, pressing the gas pedal more.

Carys glanced to her right in time to see the SUV coming but not enough to react before…

Crunch!

Chapter Eighteen

Life slowed, as though time warped and Blaize got caught in the wave.

The SUV caught him on the back right passenger side. His tires struggled to gain purchase as he spun out and then slammed into a parked car. He bit out a curse and grabbed hold of the wheel with both hands.

Fighting against momentum, he mashed the brake. His first instinct was to reach over to protect Carys, but he couldn't risk letting go of the wheel if he wanted to come out of this tailspin. If he'd been driving almost any other vehicle, it would have flipped.

Carys let out a yelp. Her hands flew to the dashboard to brace for impact. This particular model was meant for off-roading, so it had only four airbags in total, covering front-impact and seat-mounted side airbags. Despite the impact, they didn't deploy. He was thankful for small miracles and would take whatever good luck he could get. His tires seemed to be fine.

Fighting to stay in control, he finally got the Jeep to cooperate and stop spinning out. The SUV stopped. It was facing the opposite direction. He glimpsed reverse lights. Was the damn thing going to drive backward to slam into them again?

Biting back a curse, Blaize stomped on the gas pedal.

The light changed. Several vehicles turned, blocking the SUV from coming at him again.

"Are you okay?" he asked Carys, not risking taking his eyes off the road even for a second.

"I'm good." Her voice trembled. Was she in shock? Afraid?

"We'll get out of this in one piece." A trip to the police substation was a guarantee at this point. "Just a couple more blocks, right?"

"That's right," she confirmed.

"Can you grab a pic of the license plate?" he asked, figuring the law could track down the driver based on the vehicle's registration.

The drive took a few minutes. The stop cost them two hours of time. As they were being walked out, a law enforcement officer looked up from his computer screen. His nametag read: Sargeant Amber.

"We got a hit on the plate," he said, then frowned. "It was stolen from an elderly couple's vehicle while they were at the grocery. They didn't notice until one of our officers knocked on the door and asked about it." He made a sharp tic of disapproval. "Shame it didn't lead us anywhere."

"We appreciate the update, Sargeant," Blaize said. He shouldn't be surprised at the development. As much as he was convinced the person who'd attacked Carys's vehicle during the storm wasn't an experienced criminal, switching plates before chasing someone didn't take much brilliance. Or a criminal mind. The move fell into the "common sense" category. If you were going to chase someone and possibly ram your vehicle into them, you wouldn't want to advertise your home address via a license plate.

With that, he and Carys headed outside into the late-afternoon sun.

Going to the address Thomas had given them felt like stepping out of the frying pan and into the fire. Since the license was a no-lead, doing nothing meant making no progress.

"Stinks that we didn't make any progress on who is behind this," Carys said after buckling her seat.

"I know."

She rubbed the back of her neck and winced.

"Are you sure about not going to the ER to get checked out?" he asked, concerned she might still be in a mild state of shock, in which case any pain might not have kicked in yet.

"We don't have time."

"We can make time," he said.

"It wouldn't be worth the trip. I'll take ibuprofen after we eat dinner."

He opened his mouth to plead the case for going to the hospital and then clamped it shut. Panic seized him. The knot in the center of his chest tightened. He clenched his back teeth. All his systems went on high alert.

Memories of frequent hospital trips stamped his thoughts, playing out like a slideshow. Images of Lynn in wheelchair after wheelchair in various states of pain and anguish struck him like physical blows.

"I'm okay. I promise." Carys's reassurance did nothing to stem the emotional storm brewing.

After cutting on the engine, he forced an exhale and said, "Promise me one thing."

Her eyebrow shot up. "Let's hear it."

"You'll let me know if the pain worsens or you think for a second you might need to get looked at. Okay?" He couldn't count the times he'd had to respond to Lynn's screams of pain or found her flopped onto the floor because she waited too long to tell him about the pain. Thinking about it now brought on a flood of frustration and stress.

Understanding dawned. It was written on her face in the way her eyes and lips softened, and the muscles in her forehead relaxed.

She dropped her hand and reached across to touch his. "I feel a little stiff in the back of my neck from the jolt during impact. My head doesn't hurt. Just my neck. I fully believe it's temporary and will go away on its own. However, if my vision blurs or I get a headache, you'll be the first to know."

Those words brought his pulse down faster than the temperature dropping on a winter day.

"Thank you," he said to her, locking onto her gaze for a few seconds longer than was probably good for him. "You have no idea how much it means to me to hear you say that."

"Of course," she said. "And I hope you'll do the same. Tell me if anything feels off. Because I'm worried, too."

He hadn't expected that. He'd always been the "strong one" when it came to his relationship with Lynn. He'd been the one offering reassurances and sitting by her side during and after one of her episodes.

"Sounds like a fair deal to me," he said before breaking eye contact and backing out of the parking spot.

The ride to the MLK house was quiet. Not the awkward silence of strangers but two people who didn't need words between them. A lot could be said in the silence.

"I hate the fact that someone knows exactly who we are, and we have no clue about them," Carys said as he drove past the house.

"We're at a tactical disadvantage." The SUV driver had

the element of surprise. They could walk right past the person on the street and not recognize them.

Considering how busy the sidewalks in Austin usually were, MLK was a ghost town. This fact wouldn't make it easy to go unnoticed. Circling the block too many times could draw unwanted attention, so he parked instead.

Blaize exhaled. "Are you ready for this?"

So far, Carys had been attacked twice while sitting inside two different vehicles. It almost felt safer to walk outside. "We'll see in a few minutes, won't we?"

Blaize exited the driver's seat and came around to open her door. "Have I told you lately how brave you are?"

Those words stirred up more of those butterflies.

"There's a fine line between bravery and..."

"You're on the right side of the line, believe me," he said.

"Well, then, I'd like to ask for another kiss before we—"

"Done." Blaize leaned in.

Carys closed her eyes and pressed a kiss against his lips. She grabbed fistfuls of his shirt when his tongue dipped inside her mouth. She could kiss this man all day.

He broke apart first and then rested his forehead against hers, as they both took a moment to catch their breath.

"That's a lot better," she said, wishing they could go back to the hotel and just be with each other even if it wouldn't last. For once, Carys wanted to throw caution to the wind and do the thing her body craved...and right now that was Blaize. Every cell in her body craved his touch.

She'd read something about near-death experiences heightening desire. Biology wanted you to procreate as quickly as possible with the next available partner.

Were her already intense feelings toward Blaize on steroids because of this effect? Or was it something simpler than that?

Was it down to two souls who recognized each other? Who fit? Who didn't need overanalyzing to know they matched?

Could she trust it?

Could she compete with a ghost?

Shoving those thoughts aside, she reached for his hand. He immediately linked their fingers. Calm washed over her.

Without another word, they headed down the sidewalk and toward the house. She'd seen it online, walked these streets virtually, and done everything she could to prepare herself for what might happen—an ambush.

At least it was daylight and they were out in the open. While there might not have been many pedestrians, there were plenty of cars. That should help in the event of an emergency. She'd been trained to yell the word *fire* instead of *help*. Apparently people couldn't help themselves when it came to checking out a fire. They came to see if they were in danger or any of their property. Yelling *help* didn't have the same response.

She made a mental note to use the word that would draw the most attention in the event of an emergency.

"What do you say we walk past once, check our phones, and then double back like GPS misled us or was recalibrating?" he asked.

"Sounds like a good plan." Speaking of which, they didn't have one beyond getting here and checking out the house.

With every step, her pulse kicked up another notch. Her heart hammered her rib cage from the inside out. They passed the home with the yellow siding and the menacing metal bars on the front windows. No one was getting in or out that way. What were the inhabitants supposed to do if there actually was a fire?

They passed the house once, and then Blaize pulled out

his cell. He stopped. Checked the screen. Looked at her with a raised eyebrow and a shrug. Then turned back and let go of her hand long enough to point to the yellow house.

His acting deserved an award.

"Nice job," she said low and under her breath. The crash had set them back on time. They'd lost hours they needed in order to find out who Stephanie/Sharon really was and who might be after her. To find Rue's father in order to determine if he was fit to take the baby. Or, better yet, locate a next of kin who was capable of loving and caring for Rue in the manner she deserved. That would be like hitting the genetic lottery.

If someone like that existed, would Stephanie/Sharon have made arrangements? Would someone have stepped forward by now? A trusted friend? The officer who'd brought Rue to Carys had said the babysitter hadn't mentioned any known family members or friends. She'd been sitting for Rue for a short time and didn't know Stephanie very well. When she'd asked for a second emergency contact, Stephanie had said she would get back to the babysitter and then never did.

Since the cop had nothing to go on, Carys had put all her hopes on the birth-certificate angle. This was the first time she'd run into a person named on a legal document who turned out not to be the actual parent. This territory was uncharted.

Plus, she'd bent rules before, but blatantly breaking them? She was about to trespass on some random person's property in an area that looked like she would have better luck scoring drugs than getting the information they needed. Monday loomed.

Breathe.

Blaize let go of her hand as they walked up the short,

cracked concrete walkway to the pair of stairs leading to a block of concrete as a porch. He slipped away, going left. Before she could formulate words to ask what she should do, he disappeared around the corner.

Rather than just stand there, she cut right, half expecting loud, barking dogs to announce their presence. She welcomed the quiet as she searched for cameras in the eaves. If this place was some kind of drug den or human-trafficking site—her imagination was going wild at this point—wouldn't there be some type of security?

She rounded the corner on the carport side, half holding her breath. The parking space was empty. A bucket filled with cleaning supplies and a container of rags were stacked to one side. A couple of miscellaneous containers and boxes littered the back wall, some empty. Trash clung to one corner.

The place wasn't worse than many of the others she'd seen in her time at the agency. And it wasn't the best. She could tell a lot about a person by the way they kept their home. Messy was never automatically bad and meticulous wasn't always good. Hoarders always raised a red flag to her, especially when it was over the top. It signaled a mental condition that required further evaluation. Overly meticulous people who lived in wealthy neighborhoods abused their children at the same rates as folks with less financial means.

Out of the corner of her eye, she saw someone or something move in the house next door. When she turned to look, the curtain closed before she could tell who it was. A kid spying? A nosy neighbor?

She turned around the next corner, expecting to see Blaize.

He was gone.

Chapter Nineteen

Blaize circled back to the front yard where he'd left Carys. She wasn't there.

Figuring she must have circled on the carport side, he cut across the small front lawn that was sprinkled with ankle-high weeds. The property had been neglected. Same on the inside of the home, based on what he could see through one of the bedroom windows. Clothes covered old brown carpet. Empty beer and soda cans littered most surfaces. A dresser drawer sat half opened. The others were in various stages of being closed. A shirt looked to have been haphazardly flung toward the piece of bedroom furniture, landing across two drawers.

With an opened, albeit empty, pizza box wedged onto the nightstand, Blaize could only imagine how the room smelled. Or the rest of the house, for that matter. Stale beer and urine came to mind. The occupants didn't have a dog, thankfully, but he'd seen a cat curled up on top of a messy bed. *Poor thing.*

As he circled around the home toward the carport, the next-door neighbor popped out of the front door. An average-height woman in her late twenties stepped outside wearing a jean jumper and her hair in a bandana.

"Hey," Carys whispered as she headed toward him.

The neighbor held the front door open. "Can you come

here for a minute?" She glanced around nervously. "I have something to tell you about that house."

All of his protective instincts flared.

"Would you go wait in the Jeep if I asked you to?" he said to Carys.

"Doesn't seem to be any safer in it than out here," she said.

"Good point." They had just been rammed in the side by an SUV, which had disappeared as fast as it came at them. "Then stick by my side. Okay?" He reached for her hand and linked their fingers.

"Like glue," she said. "I didn't see any security cameras over here. I haven't checked the neighbor's house."

"I was on the opposite side," he said out of the corner of his mouth as they took the first steps toward the stranger.

There was no doubt that he was stronger than the tiny young woman standing on the porch, waving them on. Add Carys to the equation, and the odds that were already nil went into negative numbers.

There were unknowns. Was Bandana alone? Or was someone hiding inside the house, just out of sight? Only half of her body was visible. Was she hiding some type of weapon where they couldn't see it until it was too late? Would a vehicle come roaring up? One like the SUV?

"Hurry," Bandana said, shifting her weight back and forth while looking all around them with wide eyes. That word caused more alarm bells. If they hurried, they wouldn't have time to accurately assess the risks. "It's not safe out here."

All hope she would say what was on her mind while standing outside just died. He squeezed Carys's hand for reassurance the moment she tensed. She clearly had been thinking along the same lines.

"Please," Bandana urged as they approached the porch.

He tucked Carys behind him as they entered the living room.

Bandana shut the door behind them and locked it. Not exactly ideal, but they stood close enough for him to attack while Carys undid the lock.

"She told me to look out for you," Bandana said, staring at him. "Said if you came poking around, something bad happened to her." She brought her hand to cover her mouth as she stared.

The house was clean and cozy. More importantly, he could see straight through to the sliding glass door from his position next to the door.

"Who told you?" Carys asked before he could.

Bandana's face scrunched. "Sharon, of course."

"Had to make sure we were on the same page," she said. "I'm Carys, by the way." She was better with people than he was by a long shot.

"Rumi," she said in response.

"I'm—"

"I know who you are," Rumi said.

"Right. How?"

"Sharon gave me a message for you." She held up her index finger. "Hold on. I put it in here."

The hand-carved wooden box on the coffee table had an intricate morning-sun-over-the-mountains design.

Carys let go of his hand. "That's a beautiful box."

Rumi smiled up at Carys as she opened it. "My dad made this for me. He loved whittling. Said no one did it anymore."

Blaize resisted the urge to reach out and pull Carys back for her own safety. She was good at reading people. She knew what she was doing. She wouldn't take unnecessary risks.

So he unclenched his hands and tried not to crack a molar from biting down so hard as he let her work her magic.

"He died two years ago," Rumi said, frowning as she rooted through folded-up papers as well as the kind used to roll up a joint.

"I'm really sorry to hear that," Carys said, crouching down to eye level across the coffee table from Rumi. "Sounds like you miss him very much."

"I do," Rumi continued. "More than anyone could ever know. He was the best."

Blaize had the thought that at least someone had a decent dad. There was hope for humanity yet.

Carys was doing more than lowering Rumi's guard. She actually cared about people. It shined through in the way she interacted with them, in the questions she asked, and the way she responded. Beyond that, it came through in her mannerisms, the way she looked at you with a calm reassurance.

He experienced it every time he opened a vein and talked to her about something deeply private. Her compassion came through, making her easy to talk to. Was that the reason he'd opened up to her on such a personal level?

Rumi's eyes lit up. "Here it is. This is the note I was supposed to give you." She held it in the air. "Sharon told me that I wasn't supposed to do anything with this note except hide it unless you showed up. Is she okay?"

Blaize wasn't touching that question with a ten-foot pole. These two had obviously been close at one time.

"We're trying to figure that out right now," Carys said, not lying and not giving anything away, either. Sharon's identity had yet to be confirmed. Technically, Carys wasn't being deceptive. Plus, they needed to get out of there. The

Jeep was parked down the street. If anyone next door had anything to do with the SUV, that might be a problem.

"Can I ask how well you know your neighbor?" Carys motioned next door as Rumi handed the note over.

"Not well," Rumi said. Her frown lines deepened. "It wasn't a good place for Sharon, but she didn't go into details."

"Was there physical or mental abuse or something else like she was being trafficked?" Carys asked.

Rumi shook her head. "A bad relationship." She sat back on her heels. "You know how it goes. You meet someone you think is great, move in, and then find out how truly awful they are."

"Angel?"

"Yes, I think that's his name. I didn't see him all that much, to be honest. He works, like, two jobs and left her alone a lot. Sharon wasn't allowed to go out. He had a tracker on her phone and would call to check on her at random times so she couldn't go to the bathroom without having it on her." Her gaze bounced from Carys to Blaize and back.

"How did you two become friends?"

Rumi laughed. "We used to set the cell on the window sill and sit in the carport to talk. I'd make margaritas or we'd do tequila shots. She wore a lot of makeup to cover up the marks he left on her face."

She shook her head in disgust. The note she'd handed Blaize had been tucked inside an envelope and sealed.

An abusive ex. Was he Rue's father? No way in hell would Blaize allow a person like Angel to have custody based on what he knew about the guy so far.

"I miss her so much that I could have sworn I saw her the other day." Rumi sucked in a breath. "I'm sure it was just wishful thinking. It's been too quiet around here since she took off."

"It's hard to lose a close friend," Carys said.

Rumi looked toward the window with soft eyes and a small smile like a memory surfaced. "Can I tell you a secret?" she asked, refocusing on Carys.

"Of course," Carys said in the calmest, most reassuring tone.

"Sharon was seeing somebody else," Rumi said.

"How do you know? Is that what she told you?"

"No." Again, Rumi shook her head. Blaize got the impression she didn't get out much based on how available she'd been for Sharon and how much she seemed to need to get things off her chest even after all this time had passed since she last saw her friend. "I saw him sneaking around the back when Angel was working late."

Sharon had been having an affair? Had Angel found out?

"Did you know him?" Carys asked.

"Yeah, everyone around here does," she said like they would, too. "Silus Vexler."

"*The* Silus Vexler?" Blaize knew about the man by reputation after living in and around Austin.

"That's right."

"And you're certain about that?" he asked.

"One hundred percent," she confirmed.

That was bad.

CARYS SAT IN the passenger seat as Blaize rounded the front of the Jeep. He hadn't opened the note from Stephanie/Sharon yet. His demeanor changed the second he heard the name Silus Vexler.

"Read this to me while I drive?" he asked, holding the

note in between them. "We need to get away from this area as fast as possible."

She took the offering.

"Okay, sure. But I'm very curious as to what kind of person could cause a reaction like this in you."

"That's fair," he said. "Let's just say the SUV is the tip of the iceberg of what Silus is capable of inflicting on us."

He attempted to start the engine. Nothing.

Blaize released a string of curses. He hopped out of the vehicle and popped the hood. Poked around a few seconds before swearing again. "It's not going to start. You might as well come out."

"What happened?" She exited the passenger side.

"Someone cut the battery cables. It's not even going to start with a jump." He surveyed the area.

"Which also means someone is nearby, possibly watching us right now."

"Grab your things—we have to go." He followed her to the passenger side so she could grab her handbag from off the floorboard. She tucked the note deep inside her bag for safekeeping.

He took her hand in his and ran toward the nearest houses, aiming for in between them. The realization he was searching for cover hit hard. Losing the Jeep hit hard. And the realization a dangerous person was after them hit hardest.

Would she do all of this again for Rue? Yes. No question.

Dying wouldn't help the little girl. At least Carys understood Stephanie's dilemma now.

They made it in between two houses, away from Rumi.

"Do you think they know about Rumi?" Carys asked, trying to catch her breath as they ducked behind trash cans.

"I'm guessing they do," he said, confirming her fear

this Silus person might take out revenge on Rumi or force her to give out information about them. Fortunately, they hadn't exchanged phone numbers. They barely knew each other's identities and were on a first-name-only basis. That should protect her.

Or they might not believe her and think she was withholding information.

"We have to circle back and warn her," Carys said.

"We don't have time, and someone might already be there."

"That's what I'm afraid of," she said.

Blaize looked up at her and away from his screen. "I'm searching for a rental vehicle that's parked nearby to give us a chance to get out of here in one piece. Circling back, as much as we might want to, could put Rumi in more danger. Leaving her alone might be the best way to keep her safe." Rental cars were parked in the street and available for rent based on an app.

He was making good points. She realized that. He was being logical while she was riding on stress and emotion.

"Got one that's two blocks away," he said before locking gazes. "Say the word and we'll head back to Rumi's place. I want her to be safe as much as you do."

"But you don't like the idea of checking on her?"

"Not if it gives her information that would make someone want to torture her or draws more attention to her house," he said.

A pair of male voices that were heading toward them in a hurry made the decision for them.

"There they are," one of them said.

"We have to go," Blaize urged.

Could they make it to the car now?

Chapter Twenty

Blaize was the faster runner. However the men chasing them could have weapons. There was no choice to make. He urged Carys to run in front. This way he could put some mass—himself—in between her and those bastards.

They darted in between houses, making a big zigzag in an attempt to put more distance between the jerks and them. Whoever was chasing them stopped talking. Were these the dudes from the SUV?

It dawned on him that no one was using guns. The night of the storm, the attacker didn't break a window. Was he trying to scare Carys out of the car so he could snatch the baby? Blaize hoped like hell there wasn't some kind of reward out there for anyone who brought the kid safely to Silus. That could bring more criminals out of the woodwork—anyone looking to make a quick buck.

Damn. This thing could escalate quickly. He needed to get a hold of Raiden and bring him up to speed. Whoever followed her to the ranch the other night might have put two-and-two together.

It also dawned on him that Raiden and Kit weren't answering their phones.

Double damn.

Using the phone app, he unlocked the four-door white

sedan as they rounded the corner. It was two vehicles away, and they were coming in on the driver's side.

"Hop into the back seat to save time. Okay?" he said to Carys.

"I was just thinking the same thing," she said.

"Don't hesitate or look around—just go and then duck."

"Got it," she confirmed.

At the car, he slipped into the driver's seat and grabbed the key from underneath the mat on the floorboard. Carys hopped into the back and disappeared. They were looking for a couple, so this move might buy a few extra critical seconds needed to escape.

He started the engine and pulled out of the spot, hating leaving his Jeep behind. Since they'd tampered with his vehicle, they would be able to find his name through his registration. Fortunately, the address was still on the outskirts of Austin. Even if they had someone on the inside who could run his plate, they wouldn't get the ranch.

Hunkering down in his seat to make himself appear shorter, he navigated onto the main street that was thankfully crowded with vehicles. This was the first and only time he would see Austin traffic as a blessing instead of a curse. The white sedan was the most common color and would blend into the environment perfectly.

He glanced into the rearview and then the sideview mirrors. He scanned the vehicles around him, searching for the SUV or anyone who seemed a little too interested in everyone around them. He came up empty.

"It's probably safe for you to sit up now," he said to Carys.

"I'll stay in the back seat so, at first glance, it'll seem like you're a hired driver and I'm a fare."

"That's a good idea," he said. "It'll be safer for you to

buckle in in the event we're chased again and it's safer anyway."

She did.

"We need to get in touch with Raiden or Kit," he said, keeping a close eye on the road ahead as well as his surroundings. "I need to have my Jeep towed. I'd hate to leave it sitting out unattended. Who knows how long it'll be before I can get back to it."

"What about the note?" she asked. "Do you want me to read it now?"

With everything that had happened since leaving Rumi's, he'd tucked the note somewhere in the back of his mind. "Might as well."

"Okay. Just a sec." She fumbled around in her handbag before producing the yellowing card-sized envelope. "Here goes." She used a key to open the envelope, then pulled out a folded piece of paper. "Are you ready?"

The secret of how Stephanie/Sharon knew him was about to be revealed. "I guess so."

"It says, 'You probably won't remember me even if you see me again. I'm going red instead of blond, and I'm changing the way I make up my face. I overheard you talking about losing your wife, Lynn, at Deep Roots, and I knew right then and there you were the person I wanted to take care of my baby. I'm starting to show and have to get out of my situation before it's too late and he knows. Anyway, you seem like a nice guy. Like the kind of person my Lark deserves. I've made mistakes. Big ones. But I'll figure something out. If I don't, well, I guess you came looking for answers like I hoped you would. Don't be mad. Whatever happens, please don't let him get hold of her.'"

"There's only one other person I mentioned Lynn to, and that was at Deep Roots not long after she died."

"Guess Sharon was there, too," Carys said.

"Seems so," he said.

"Who is this man anyway?"

"You haven't heard of Silus Vexler?" He figured everyone knew the man, or to avoid him at the very least.

"Why? Should I?"

"His name gets around in Austin for leaning on business owners for so-called protection," he said.

"I didn't realize that was a thing," she admitted. "I just went to school here. I moved away when I got the job in Maverick Pass."

"That's possibly why you would never have crossed paths with him. I used to manage a custom saddle business, and my suppliers had trouble with him since they sourced across the border. I knew he was bad news, but he didn't come knocking on my door."

"Do you still work there?"

"No. After Lynn passed, I spiraled. Went to a dark place. Gave up my job because I couldn't go into work every day and pretend everything was fine. My employees deserved better."

"Do you mind if I ask how you survived financially?"

"By that point, I had stock in the company. Sold most of it to pay for Lynn's treatments that insurance decided not to cover. There was enough left over to live on for a while. That's what I've been doing." He choked out a laugh. "Funny thing about it is that I was about to head back to work. Finally got my head on straight and decided it was time to make some money, pick my life up and find a way to move forward. Then I got the call about Cormac dying. Seems like every time I set off in a direction, the universe laughs and throws me a new twist." He would have said it always went from bad to worse, but then he met her. He couldn't regret that one bit. It also brought him Rue. "If I changed my mind and told you that I'm the little girl's father, would you believe me?"

She sat in silence for a long moment, giving away nothing. Before she could answer, his cell buzzed.

"Can you answer that for me?" he asked.

"Sure." She leaned forward enough to grab the phone from the cupholder. "It's Raiden."

"THIS IS CARYS. I have you on speaker."

"Blaize? Are you there, too?" The concern in Raiden's voice caused her pulse to race. Rue was crying softly in the background.

"I'm here," Blaize said. "I'm driving, so Carys is helping me out."

Raiden exhaled.

"Is everything okay? Because when no one answered and I didn't hear back from you, I was worried something happened," Blaize said, getting right to the point.

"It's Kit."

Blaize's knuckles turned white on the steering wheel. "What about her?"

"She fell."

"Again?"

"I'm afraid so," Raiden said. "Caught the corner of the dresser this time and had to get stitches."

"Where are you guys now?"

"At the hospital." The strain in Raiden's voice said it had been a long day in Maverick Pass, too.

"Is Kit conscious?" Blaize asked.

"Yes."

"Is that Rue crying in the background?"

"Yes." He cleared his throat. "A nurse is helping me try

to calm her so I could call you. The kid has a set of lungs on her, and I'm not cut out to be a parent. I've tried everything I know to do, which isn't a helluva a lot, and none of it works."

All of a sudden, Rue stopped crying.

"What just happened?" Blaize asked.

"The nurse swaddled her."

"Did you change her diaper?" Blaize asked.

"Yes."

"Feed her?"

"Did that, too."

"Does she have a fever?" Blaize asked.

All these questions were spot-on. Carys had no clue why Blaize didn't think he'd be a good father. Now that she knew his background and about his wife, was he afraid to admit he still wanted children?

It would be understandable after all the disappointments he'd endured. Most people would have folded the tent at this point. Not Blaize. He became stronger and more determined with every setback.

"The nurse checked. No, no fever."

"That's a relief." Blaize released some of the tension in his grip on the steering wheel.

"There doesn't seem to be a reason for her to be fussy," Raiden said. "And Kit will be fine, by the way."

"Will she?" Blaize asked.

"She says this is the reason we have to sell and put her in a home."

"And you believe her?"

"I can only go by what she says." Raiden sounded at the end of his rope. He also sounded much less confident than he had when he first arrived. A good sign?

"We're heading back now," Blaize said. "Is Kit being released tonight?"

"That's the plan, according to her doctor."

"Keep me posted, will you?" Blaize frowned. "There's not much I can do from the road, but I'll be there as soon as humanly possible."

"Will do." Raiden paused a beat. "Any guesses as to your ETA?"

"I'm three hours out, if traffic cooperates." He didn't mention the fact they could be derailed by someone determined to take them out. Was it safe to go back to the ranch?

They couldn't leave Rue with Kit and Raiden anymore.

The brothers exchanged goodbyes. Their bond might have been challenged, but Carys could hear how much they cared for each other in their voices. You can't fake something as genuine as that. She'd witnessed people trying to convince her they were a solid unit. She had a special detector for people like that.

"What if whoever cut my battery cable gets to them first?" Blaize said the minute the call ended.

She glanced at the screen to make certain Raiden didn't accidentally hear something he shouldn't. Relief washed over her when the generic screensaver came up. "Everyone should be safe at the hospital."

"What if Kit is released before we get there?"

"That's a possibility. But there's a good chance we'll get there first." The mention of hospitals caused Blaize's muscles to string tight. Having his beloved Kit in one must be the worst feeling.

"There is so much that needs to be done when I get back." He rubbed the two-day-old scruff on his chin. Dark circles cradled his eyes, and yet the man was still sex-on-a-stick gorgeous, looking more like a sculpture than a human.

Carys faked a cough. "I seem to be coming down with something. I could take a couple of days off, just until you get settled. Besides, I need to make a trip to the orphanage to explain why I kept Rue over the weekend."

"Will you have to drop her off?"

"At some point she—"

He gave one finite headshake. "If you don't get me busted for not being her father, the government believes I'm the one at least for now. Correct?"

"I have to establish paternity at some point in the near future. I can't leave it open-ended like this and keep my job. Plus, my boss will catch on and the courts will require proof before establishing custody."

"I'll find a way to adopt her. I'll get a lawyer to intervene. I'll say her mother was my best friend and wanted me to be the guardian."

"Blaize, be reasonable. You can't take care of everyone. Kit needs someone in the house to watch over her. Rue is a full-time job. You heard how tired Raiden is. It's already too much. Add in the fact you need to save the ranch to keep a roof over Kit's head and there's just too much going on for you to be able to take care of an infant."

"I can do it."

Stubborn must've been his middle name. Carys admired his determination. Reality said that he wasn't Superman.

"If anyone could, it would be you." She needed to add a dose of reality into the situation. "The task is impossible, and you would wear yourself down. I can help for a couple of days, but then I'll have to get back to my own schedule. Where does that leave Rue?"

"I need that meeting with my brothers to figure it out. What if they come back? What if everyone takes a shift? We have to have someone home to watch Kit while she's awake anyway. Why not let them assist her in taking care of Rue?"

"That sounds more like a fairy tale than reality."

He bit down on his bottom lip. "Having Rue in the house has made Kit the happiest I've seen her. They always say parents never recover from losing a child. Cormac wasn't a kid, but he was her son and she loved him. So much so, she jumped to his defense when I brought up one or two of his many deficiencies. I barely scratched the surface."

"She loves you, too."

"I guess I can do no wrong in her eyes. Believe me when I say I'm far from perfect." He glanced around. "I can pull over if you want to slide up to the passenger seat."

"It might be safer to stay like this for a while even though we're on the highway now."

"Let me know if you change your mind," he said.

"Okay." She thought about what he said about Kit. "I highly doubt my father would care if I lived or died. It's too bad not every parent is like Kit, protective even when their kids make huge mistakes."

"She's special," he agreed. "Do you think you'll reconnect with your father at some point?"

"Why? So he can remind me how much I disappointed him? Or tell me again that I'm not his daughter? That one stung at eighteen."

Blaize was quiet for a long moment. Based on the wrinkle across his forehead, he was deep in thought. "I would have liked the chance to tell Cormac what a disappointment he was to his face and how much it damaged us growing up. Now? I'll never get the chance."

"I thought you were going to tell me to try to reconcile with my father," she said. His words resonated.

"What would be the point of that?" he asked. The question was rhetorical. "It's far better to be able to reconcile with yourself. Does that make any sense?"

"Actually, yes. It does. A whole lot of sense, actually." When this ordeal was over, could she reach out? Tell her father how she really felt about the way he'd treated her for wanting to live her own life?

Could she open up to Blaize, too? Risk losing him and Rue?

Chapter Twenty-One

The call came when they were twenty minutes away from the hospital. A nurse had agreed to help get Rue strapped into her car seat safely for the ride home since she held certification as a car seat safety tech. The amount of relief in Raiden's voice when Blaize said they would arrive home at close to the same time was almost comical.

"Did you hear that?" he asked Carys.

She laughed, and he'd be damned if it wasn't the most musical sound. Now that he was determined to keep Rue, would Carys bolt at the first opportunity?

His problems were mounting. The last thing he needed to think about was Carys leaving. Or the kisses they'd shared, which had been the highlight of his year, possibly his life.

How was that for being dramatic?

Blaize chuckled. Too much stress had him on the edge, imagining that his heart would shatter when she walked out.

Didn't everyone leave?

Whoa! Did he really believe that? Or was it just his mind searching for reasons to counter what his heart so plainly saw…that Carys was special.

"How could I miss it? Your poor brother is in way over his head and knows it. At least Rue was quiet this time. I felt even worse for him when she was crying." Carys stilled in the back seat. She'd stayed put the whole ride.

Did he have the same feelings for him or was he latching onto something that wasn't there? His mind was clear. He knew what he wanted. And then the universe laughed and threw every possible obstacle in his way.

When he thought about it on a practical level, how was he supposed to save a ranch, take care of Kit, and bring up a baby? Adding a relationship on top seemed impossible.

He was getting ahead of himself. First, he had to convince his brothers that saving the ranch was a good idea. If they refused to move back and pitch in, he would have to figure out a way to do it all himself.

Easy-peasy.

Blaize almost laughed out loud. Was he losing his mind?

Probably.

He parked at the house. Carys exited the car before he did.

"I need to make a work call," she said, walking away. "Do you mind?"

"Stick close enough to see me, just in case."

She gave a quick nod and walked out of earshot. Was she calling her boss? He didn't like the idea of her getting into trouble because of him. If he'd lied about being Rue's father from the get-go, they wouldn't be in this mess.

Not true. The person would have attacked her car. She might still be in trouble.

He kept one eye on her as he stood up and stretched his legs. Working out had been a lifesaver while Lynn was sick. Ranch work would give him plenty of physical labor.

It dawned on him that a screwworm had been reported to be infecting cows across the border. In response, supplies were being cut off so as not to infect cattle here. And that was a longwinded way of saying he could sell at a better price if he took cattle to market now. He'd never seen prices so high. Could a sale buy him some time to straighten out finances on the ranch? Allow him to hire help for Kit, if needed? It was worth a shot.

Carys ended the call, tucked the phone inside her handbag, and frowned as she walked toward him. "That didn't go well."

"What happened?"

"My boss knows about Rue. Called me out for saying I was sick. Told me to take the time away to make sure my priorities are straight." She exhaled and pinched the bridge of her nose. "So, basically, I'm on leave now until I refocus and I have to take Rue to the orphanage tonight. My boss said she would be checking to make sure Rue is at Sister's Love before bed check."

"When is that?" He needed a minute to process and come up with a plan.

"A couple of hours," she said.

Damn.

"I just had a thought," he said. "What if Rue is safer at the orphanage than with us for the time being?"

"It's been hard enough leaving her for the day. How am I supposed to drop her off and walk away?" The hurt and disappointment in her eyes stabbed him. She was right. Being away from Rue had been more difficult than he'd anticipated. The only reason he could fathom leaving her at Sister's Love for the night was due to it being safer than the ranch. Would he worry? Hell yes.

"I know what you mean," he said.

"Plus, if the people who are after us figure us out, they might be tracking our movements," she continued.

"Sure," he said. Every which way they turned, there was risk involved. Their next step would have to be about taking the least-dangerous path. “So far, they haven’t tried to shoot at us, which I take to mean they don’t want to risk hurting the baby.”

“If these bastards are trying to collect a reward or get in good with the head honcho, they can’t bring in damaged goods.” She quickly added, “I don’t see her that way, but she’s nothing but a means to an end for them.”

“They don’t want to get caught,” he reasoned. “Isn’t there security cameras or some form of failsafe at the orphanage?”

“It’s a small place that’s out of the way of the mainstream. I doubt they’d do much more than lock the doors and expect to be safe.”

“We can go there to investigate. If it doesn’t feel right, we’ll turn around and bring her back here.”

Carys bit down on her lower lip. “I can live with that.”

“I’ll see if Raiden can stay the night since we can’t leave Kit alone.”

The crunch of gravel underneath tires and the hum of an engine didn’t normally cause his blood pressure to rise. Until he saw it was just his brother’s vehicle coming up the path, his stress levels doubled.

Raiden pulled up next to Blaize and parked. Carys immediately went to Rue. She opened the door to the back on the passenger side and unbuckled the carrier.

“Where’s your Jeep?” Raiden asked.

“Long story,” Blaize said. They had a little time before they needed to get Rue to the orphanage. “I’ll tell you over a cup of coffee and a bite of food.”

“I’m starving,” Carys said, holding on to the baby carrier for dear life. The determined and protective expression on her face said she’d fight anybody who tried to take Rue away.

Rue was lucky to have someone like Carys in her corner.

He focused on helping Kit out of the car. "You gave us another scare. Is there something you're not telling me about a medical condition?"

"Hogwash," Kit said. "I'm peachy."

"Two falls in two days say otherwise." He lowered his voice to a gentler tone.

"All the more reason to sell this place, so you can put me in a home." There was no conviction in those words.

"Are you trying to leave me all alone?"

Raiden opened the back door and let them inside.

"You'll be better off," Kit said. "I'm a burden at this point."

"Like hell you are." He wouldn't let her get away with making it seem like she'd be doing him a favor. "You happen to be one of my favorite people in the world. How could you be anything but amazing?"

Fears she was hiding a serious—terminal?—medical condition intensified. How the hell would he do any of this without Kit?

CARYS CHANGED RUE'S diaper and fed her as Blaize and Raiden prepared a meal. Kit sat at the kitchen table, nursing a glass of water. She'd done a number on her forehead, come home with wound-care instructions that Blaize had her go over with all three of them in the room.

Her heart went out to the baby. With no other relatives and a dry well of foster families, Rue was most likely going to have to spend the night at the orphanage.

Since beating herself up wasn't productive, she started thinking up ways to keep a close eye on Rue. Could she volunteer at the orphanage? She had connections. She knew the director. There was no way she could ask her boss to give them a call and make the recommendation. Still, as a CPS agent, her background had already been picked apart and processed. No job was too small. She would be willing to do janitorial work if it meant being close to Rue until Carys could come up with a plan.

It was too late to redact her statement about Blaize denying paternity. Was it even possible for him to gain custody of Rue without actually taking a paternity test, a test he would surely fail?

After he shared the state of his finances, hiring a hotshot lawyer would be out of the question. She would contribute funds if she had anything left over. Paying living expenses and student loans took a good chunk of her income every month.

It's fine. It'll be fine. Everything is fine. How many times had she repeated the mantra growing up? It had gotten her through difficult years. She could only hope it still held some of its magic.

"Dinner smells good," Kit said, interrupting Carys's thoughts. "What are you boys cooking up?"

Raiden brought over a tray and set it on the table. "Cowboy Chili on Fritos."

Blaize brought over bowls and spoons.

"I thought chili had to slow-cook all day," Carys said.

Raiden laughed. "We have a cheat code to speed it up. Basically, we just doctor already-made chili from the can." He dipped a spoon inside the large bowl and scooped up a Frito before handing it over. "Taste it for yourself."

Rue was asleep in Carys's arms. She tried to finagle taking the spoon.

"Here, let me help." Blaize took over and fed her a bite.

"Mmm. That's amazing."

His self-satisfied smile shouldn't have been as sexy as

it was. What could she say? She would never get tired of seeing that man smile or the effect it had on her.

"Do you want me to hold her while you eat?" Blaize asked.

"I'm just scared that if I set her down, I'll never get to hold her again. Is that weird?"

Heads shook around the table as each person offered a look of understanding.

"I'll just put her in her carrier." It was on the floor sitting right next to her. She could eat and keep one eye on the baby. Blaize took a seat on the other side of the carrier, with Rue in between them.

Carys glanced around at the faces at the table as tears welled in her eyes. She blinked them back as she realized this was the first real family meal she'd experienced. An ache formed in her chest as a picture of these people eating dinner with her every evening took form. It caught her off guard how natural it felt and how easily conversation flowed.

Blaize got his brother up to speed over the meal. They traded playful barbs, which thankfully lightened the mood. Kit piped in every once in a while with a quip of her own, making everyone laugh. It was easy to see why Blaize loved his grandmother so much.

The meal ended too soon. It was time to take Rue to the orphanage.

"I should probably give her a bath before we leave." Was she stalling for time? Hell yes.

"That's a good idea," Kit offered.

The prospect of figuring out how to bathe a baby must've contorted her face based on the way everyone looked at her.

"I can help," Kit said. "I used to be quite the hand at taking care of these little ones."

"Is it a good idea for you to get up?" Carys asked, concerned.

"Those doctors can't tell me what to do," the woman quipped. She pushed up to standing. "See, I'm as fit as a fiddle and sharp as a tack."

The way she'd mentioned the word *doctors* raised alarm bells for Carys. Given everything Blaize had been through, his mind must've been running wild with possibilities. The stress cracks on his forehead said everything she needed to know. He was worried. She didn't blame him.

Kit refocused on Carys. "Are you ready to give that little sweetheart a bath?"

"Yes, I am."

Carys was grateful for the help. She didn't have the first clue of how to take care of a baby. Did you run bath water? That didn't seem right. Did you put them in the sink? No, probably not. Having someone with experience around would keep Carys from panicking.

"Let's take her into the bedroom so we can put her on a soft surface," Kit said.

Carys took note of the way Kit held on to her arm, half guiding, half using it to steady herself. They walked into the guest bedroom where Kit had been sleeping. Carys put the carrier down on the floor.

"We'll need a towel and a washcloth from the bathroom," Kit said.

"Got it."

She returned with both in a matter of seconds.

"Let's put the towel on top of the comforter and spread it out."

Carys did.

"I'll let you pick Rue up since I'm not so steady on my feet these days." Kit sounded more than a little frustrated.

"What did the ER doctor say is happening?" Carys asked as she unbuckled Rue and then put her on top of the towel.

"Inner-ear infection," Kit said. "He wants me to take antibiotics, but I refuse."

"Why is that?"

"They make me too sick," she said. "I'm sure it'll clear up on its own."

"Blaize is worried about you falling again," Carys said. "What if I call your doctor and get a different prescription?"

"There is one that'll help, but it's not covered under insurance," Kit explained. "Blaize has enough on his mind without trying to come up with two hundred dollars on the spot."

"Where is the prescription being held?"

"Pharmacy in town. Why?"

"Just curious." Carys would pay for it out of her own pocket. She also wondered if this was the reason Kit kept pushing to sell. "This land is amazing."

"House needs fixin' up." Based on Kit's tone, Carys struck a chord.

"Nothing a few boards, nails, and paint can't handle."

"Blaize has already sacrificed too much," Kit said. "I wouldn't ask him to do more. He's suffered enough."

"He might suffer more if you don't let him take care of this place. And you."

"My grandson looks like he's aged ten years in the past two. Now I know why."

"He's been through more than his fair share," Carys said. "But he's strong."

Kit's chin came up, proud. "He sure is."

"And you believe in him, don't you?"

"I sure do."

"Then maybe let him fix this place up and get it running again," Carys said. "It'll do him good to see the results."

Kit studied Carys like she was looking through her to the core of who she was.

"He's different with you," she said. "It's the first time I've seen him happy."

What was Carys supposed to do with that?

Chapter Twenty-Two

Blaize parked in the lot next to a pickup at Sister's Love. He exited the rental car and opened the door for Carys. Working like a team, they freed the carrier from the seat belt and grabbed the diaper bag. Rue had been in his life for less than forty-eight hours yet had managed to imprint his heart. If he lost her, he would regret it for the rest of his life.

Sister's Love was in need of TLC, much like the ranch. Two stories with peeling paint, it had an almost ominous air to it. The wraparound porch had seen better days. Once he got the ranch up and running again, he could gather a group of volunteers to work on this place.

As they approached the door, it opened from the inside. A short, round woman welcomed them inside.

"I'm Rosie," she said to Blaize. "I'd offer a handshake but yours are full. Can I take her from—"

"Could we sit down for a minute?" Carys asked.

"Of course." Rosie led them from the foyer into a formal living area. The furniture looked to be original to the house. She held out her hand toward the sofa. "Please, sit down."

"I know how challenging it has been with staffing," Carys said, starting right in. "I'd like to volunteer for the next couple of days."

Rosie blinked like she couldn't believe her eyes. "We're

always looking for good people. You of all people know that. We'd love to have you. I'll get the paperwork started tomorrow morning."

"I was thinking more like starting tonight," Carys said.

"With paperwork? Nothing can be done until—"

"I know you need the help, Rosie. And I don't feel good about dropping her off and running when I know how short-staffed you are."

"I appreciate your willingness to drop everything else in your life and help." Rosie sat up a little straighter. "I can assure that we can handle every situation that comes through that door."

"You sure about that?"

Carys's words landed like bullets.

Rosie stood up, shot a glare, and grabbed the handle to the carrier. The hallway was too dark to make anything out clearly. Blaize saw the outline of someone lingering. Was she waiting to take Rue?

"Hold on, Rosie. I didn't mean it to come out like that." Carys's tone was pleading.

Blaize reached over and took her hand in his. It was then he realized hers was trembling. Watching Rosie take Rue away and hand her off hit hard.

Carys stood. He followed suit. She squeezed his fingers.

The baby was then given to the silhouette.

Rosie turned around, blocking their view of the hallway. "Shall I walk you out, or do you want me to call the authorities?"

"There's no need to do anything like that," Blaize said, a little shocked at the threat. "We're heading out now."

Carys hesitated. He squeezed her hand gently for reassurance. Thankfully, she followed him out the front door without an argument. The last thing they needed to do tonight was get the sheriff involved. Carys didn't need another hit on her performance record.

"We'll figure something out," he said as soon as they were in the clear and walking toward the rental car.

Out of the corner of his eye, he saw a streak of red behind the building.

Nah. Couldn't be.

What the hell?

"I think she's here," Blaize said.

"Who?" Carys's forehead wrinkled with confusion. And then it dawned on her. Her mouth snapped open and shut. "Sharon?"

He signaled toward the back of the house. Then took off running.

The front door opened, and Rosie came out in a hurry. "Carys. Don't leave yet. Can I speak to you?"

TORN BETWEEN FOLLOWING Blaize and hearing what Rosie had to say, Carys froze.

"Go talk to her," Blaize said before disappearing around back.

"What is it?"

"She was here," Rosie said, waving Carys inside. "Please. Hurry."

Carys jogged over and then followed Rosie into the house, stopping in the foyer. "What's going on, Rosie?"

The woman twisted her fingers together. Beads of sweat formed on her forehead. "There was a man with a gun. He had her."

"Who?"

"Sharon."

"You know her?" Carys didn't bother to hide her shock.

"She came here when she was pregnant," Rosie admitted, working her fingers. "We let her help out off the record. She said she was in trouble and needed our help."

"Blaize just saw red hair," Carys said, trying to process what she was hearing.

"She dyed it so the baby's father wouldn't recognize her."

"You knew all of this and didn't say anything?"

"I helped a pregnant single mother without quizzing her," Rosie said. "It's part of what we do here."

"We have reason to believe she died in a car crash."

"No." Rosie shook her head. "That would be impossible because she was taken out the back door after you handed over the baby."

"You took Rue and delivered her to a criminal," Carys said, her tone accusatory.

"I gave her to her mother." Rosie compressed her lips into a frown. "And now I have no idea what to do."

"Call the sheriff and explain everything you just told me," Carys said.

"Sharon said he would kill her if I did that," she admitted.

"I have to go." Carys started toward the back door. "Blaize is out there. Alone."

A shot fired.

Oh no.

Carys's heart dropped. Rosie grabbed hold of her. The world started to spin. Nausea caused bile to rise up and burn the back of her throat.

Blaize!

"Don't go out there," Rosie said. "You might end up getting shot."

"I can't leave Blaize out there alone to deal with—"

The back door opened so hard it smacked against the wall. Rosie screamed.

"It's me," Blaize said.

Carys bolted around her and into the dark hallway toward the kitchen. The first thing she saw was blood.

"Blaize, you're shot."

"I know. It's okay." It would be just like him to reassure her when he was the one bleeding out. "It's not as bad as it looks."

Blood flowered on his shirt sleeve near his right bicep.

"It's a lot of blood, Blaize."

He was shot, bleeding. Rue was gone. Sharon was somehow alive.

"Help me!" shouted a female voice from outside.

Rosie came running into the kitchen and straight to the door. "It's her."

"Don't open that door," Carys warned. "It could be a trap."

But it was too late. Rosie had already undone the lock. The second she did, the door flung open and smacked her.

"Rosie," the redhead from the picture—Sharon—said with concern in her voice. She scanned the room. "I'm so sorry."

"Where's the baby?" Carys asked.

"He got her," Sharon said.

"We have to get her back. Call the sheriff," Carys said to Rosie. "Now!"

"They'll arrest me," Sharon said.

"Do you want to lose Rue forever?" Carys worked on stemming the blood dripping down Blaize's elbow.

"Who has her?" he asked.

"Silus," Sharon said.

"He came himself?" Blaize asked. He looked to Carys. "I've got this." She'd put enough pressure to stop the bleeding temporarily.

"That's right. He said he couldn't trust anyone else to get the job done or handle a precious package like her and—"

"Lock the door behind me," Blaize said. "I know a shortcut. I can head him off, but I have to go now."

"Not in this condition, you can't." No way was Carys letting him go out there without her. "You're bleeding."

He shrugged it off like it was nothing.

"Then I'm coming."

"Too risky."

She shot her best *do not argue with me* look and followed him out the back door after he heaved a sigh and then jumped into action. The lock snicked the moment they were outside. Good that Rosie took it seriously. Not so good that they couldn't turn around and go back inside if Silus was out here.

Blaize took off running toward a wooded area. She did her best to keep up as she fumbled with her cell. Rosie might not call law enforcement due to Sharon's request, but Carys had no problem doing it. If the woman ended up in jail, so be it. For Rue's sake, Carys hoped the courts would go easy on Sharon.

Silus was a different story altogether. That man needed to rot in a burning—

Dammit.

Carys dropped her cell. It was black as pitch out here. There was no way she could keep going and find it.

"Do you have your phone on you?" she asked Blaize as they half hopped, half ran through scrub brush, zigzagging in and out of trees. Branches slapped her face and torso as they bolted through the woods.

They ran long past her thighs burning. She was lost. It was dark. What if they ended up stuck out here overnight?

The shock of seeing Sharon alive and of Blaize being shot was something she might never recover from.

A glimpse of red taillights stopped Blaize so fast that Carys ran into his back.

As they moved closer, a familiar sound pierced her chest like a bullet through armor. Rue's cries broke Carys's heart.

From this distance, they could see that the driver's-side door was open. Had he fled, leaving his daughter to fend for herself?

The question they should have asked was *Why would Silus abandon the vehicle?* They didn't. Emotion overtook logic when it came to Rue.

"Stay here," Blaize warned.

"Like hell I will."

Carys bolted around Blaize on his right side and ran like hell toward Rue.

Chapter Twenty-Three

Anything that happened next would be on Blaize. He shouldn't have brought Carys out here into the thicket. He shouldn't have gone after Silus half-cocked with no weapon or plan. And he shouldn't have let Carys get past him just now.

She'd chosen his injured side, so he couldn't stop her from running toward Rue. He couldn't blame Carys. He wanted to do the exact same thing.

It wasn't the best move.

He winced as he expected to hear another round being fired. Either way, he wouldn't wait. He took off after Carys and toward the abandoned vehicle.

The engine idled.

Silus had taken off in a hurry. What did that mean?

The answer came in the form of a downed tree lying across the road, blocking it. There was no way the vehicle could drive over it. He could have in his Jeep. But Silus would never get the sedan over the massive trunk.

Maybe his luck was turning. He'd had enough bad luck to last a lifetime. Were the powers that be finally giving him a break?

Carys got to the vehicle first. The loss of blood made him dizzy and move slower. He was halfway there when the crack of a bullet split the air. The world stilled, and everything moved in slow motion.

Carys dropped to the ground. Hit?

He instinctively dove for cover, then army-crawled toward her despite the biting pain in his arm.

"Did it..."

He couldn't manage to finish the question. Then he didn't need to. She rolled onto her side, and he saw a red dot flowering on her upper thigh.

Blaize cursed the heavens and earth.

He immediately stripped off his shirt.

"No. You need that," she said, eyes wide in a state of mild shock.

"You need it more." If they didn't stem the bleeding, she might bleed out. Now that he'd found her, he couldn't lose her. Not her, too.

He wrapped the shirt around her thigh slightly above the wound and tightened the knot enough to slow the bleeding, if not stop it altogether. "Let's get you in the back seat."

Could he hop into the front and turn this vehicle around? Head back to the house?

There wasn't much of a choice, was there? Neither of them were in any condition to run back to the house. Add the weight of carrying the baby and it would be next to impossible.

The nagging question of why Silus abandoned the car and baby niggled at the back of his mind. All he could focus on right now was getting the three of them to safety.

He helped Carys into the back. "Stay down. Okay?"

"Okay," she parroted.

Another nagging question surfaced. Why only one shot? They were out in the open. Did Silus know he'd hit both his targets and figured it was a matter of time before they bled out? Problem solved without even having to get his hands dirty? Or was he saving bullets until he could get in closer range in case he'd missed?

Would he panic and take off? The shots meant to stop anyone from following? Silus wasn't normally the one to get his hands dirty, was he?

Blaize took the driver's seat and closed the door. He sank as low as possible into the seat, not bothering to put on his seat belt. The smaller the target he made, the better.

Rather than turn the vehicle around, he put the gearshift in reverse and sped backward until it seemed safe. Only then did he turn the vehicle around for the rest of the drive to the house. The only other road meant driving by the house again. So be it.

"How are you doing back there?" he asked Carys.

Rue had stopped crying, and it was far too quiet in the back seat as far as he was concerned. He glanced at the rearview. Carys's head was lying against the headrest, bobbling back and forth on the gravelly road.

"I'm okay," she said, her voice weak.

Could he get back to the house and call for emergency medical treatment? Or should he risk getting on the road? There were probably some supplies back at the house. Had the makeshift torniquet's knot come loose? Had the bullet hit an artery?

"Stay with me," he said to her, more plea than request. "I can't lose you, Carys. I love you." He risked a glance. "You should know that I've fallen in love with you and I can't imagine spending another minute without you."

He couldn't lose Carys.

Did she hear him?

Was she conscious?

The fact she hadn't responded made the decision to stop

at the house clear. She might not make it to the hospital. At the house, she had a fighting chance.

He couldn't lose Carys.

Blaize sped to Sister's Love. He pulled up in front, not bothering to park. He couldn't get out of the driver's seat fast enough. He immediately pulled Carys from the car. Her head fell to one side. No. Not a good sign.

He couldn't lose Carys.

The front door opened, and Rosie stumbled onto the porch. Eyes wide, mouth open, her look of shock and sudden jerk forward said she was pushed from behind. Sharon came out next in similar fashion.

And then Silus came partially into view. He stood behind the ladies.

"Turn your head," he said to Sharon.

She winced as he forced her to comply, revealing that he had the barrel of a gun pressed to the back of her head. The redhead was crying as she mouthed the words *I'm sorry.*

She couldn't have known any of this was going to happen. Blaize couldn't blame her for trying to survive and make a better life for her child.

A desperate person took desperation actions.

"Give us the baby and walk away," Silus said.

"The woman with me needs medical care, or she's going to die," Blaize said. "If she dies, that makes you a murderer."

"Hand over the baby," Silus said, his voice reaching an almost hysterical pitch. The man was agitated.

Sharon subtly shook her head and mouthed the word *no.*

"Do as I say, or I'll shoot you both," Silus demanded.

"How should we do this?" Blaize asked.

"Get her out of my car and step away," he said. "I'll take it from there."

"How do you plan to get out of this, Silus? What comes next?" Blaize realized the man wouldn't want to leave witnesses. There were four, with himself and Carys being the wild cards in the equation. "This hasn't gone so far that you can't walk away. Let me get her inside and stop the bleeding before it's too late."

"Once you step away from the vehicle, you can do anything you want. Now, do what I said or I'll start shooting beginning with Sharon."

"You don't want to shoot the mother of your child," Blaize warned. If he did as Silus asked, the man could disappear with Sharon and the baby into his criminal network. The two might not surface for years, if they did at all. He would likely shoot Rosie if he took her along for the ride. Dump the body somewhere it might never be found.

Silus was known for pressuring business owners into paying protection money. He had enough ties to thugs to hide behind them for ages. He could skip across the border, run his business from there. Force Sharon to live in horror with the threat of taking her daughter away.

No wonder she disappeared, changed her name, and then tried to fake her death. At some point, CPS would have linked Stephanie to Sharon, Rue would be in safe hands—his!—and then Sharon could have come back to retrieve her daughter once the dust settled. She could have started a new life in another place.

"I said now!" Silus was growing more desperate.

This wasn't good.

"Okay, just give me a minute to get her out of the car safely," he said, stalling for time. Once Silus got everyone into the car, it would be much easier to slip away and disappear. The law didn't have a great track record of shutting the man's business down. No, Silus had figured out how to get around the legal system. He knew how to fly under the radar, using others to do the heavy lifting for him.

At this point, Sharon would likely testify under oath that she wanted to go with Silus of her own free will. The shooting could be chalked up to accidents. Who the hell knew what this man was capable of pulling off.

Slowly, carefully, he wrapped arms around Carys and gently pulled her from the vehicle.

Her eyes opened for a few seconds, locking onto his. Was she conscious?

He could have sworn she winked at him, but he was probably just seeing what he wanted to instead of the reality that he was losing her with every second that ticked by.

Silus knocked Sharon forward another step. Rosie gasped.

"Shut the hell up, woman, or I'll shoot every last one of you." The threat rang hollow to Blaize. Silus couldn't afford to shoot everyone, but Rosie panicked. She brought her hand up to cover her mouth and tried to step away.

He pistol-whipped her across the cheek. The older woman let out a pitiful yelp.

"Don't hurt her," Sharon said, panicked. "I'll do whatever you want, but leave Rosie out of this."

"That woman kept you from me while you were carrying my child," Silus bit out through clenched teeth. "She doesn't deserve to—"

"Please, Silus," Sharon begged. "She didn't know that I was your girl."

Those last two words were fingernails on a chalkboard to Blaize. First of all, Sharon was not a girl, she was a grown woman. And secondly, she didn't belong to anyone except herself.

The trio moved toward them. Silus kept the gun firmly pointed to the back of Sharon's head. Based on the panic in her eyes, he would shoot if pushed too far.

Blaize held Carys in his arms, taking another step back.

"Move," Silus insisted.

Blaize took another step. He was too far away to make a move without risking Silus accidently squeezing the trigger mechanism. He bit back a few choice words.

"Get in first," Silus said to Rosie, kicking her as she turned toward the back driver's-side door. It was still open, and there was blood on the seat and floorboard. At least they were leaving a DNA trail that would be next to impossible to cover. *If* the police could catch up to Silus before he torched the vehicle.

It dawned on Blaize why Sharon would have "died" in a fiery crash. The fire would erase all DNA evidence. It also made the driver impossible to positively ID. If Sharon wasn't in the vehicle, who was? Did she murder someone? Drug them and then set the car ablaze?

Sharon might end up in jail for murder the rest of her life when Blaize turned Silus in. Where would that leave Rue?

As Silus passed by, Carys's body seized. For a split second, Blaize feared she might be dying, but then she opened her eyes and was surprisingly lucid.

Her foot, however, landed on Silus's ribs. She kicked so hard, he flew into the driver's-side door. Caught by surprise, the gun flew out of his hand.

Sharon screamed, processed what had just happened, and before Silus could regain his balance, she went wild on him, kicking and punching and screaming.

Carys bucked out of Blaize's arms. As much as he tried to balance her, she still landed on the ground half on her side. Something cracked. Her wrist, maybe, as she planted her hand down to break her fall.

The time to act was now or never.

Chapter Twenty-Four

Carys landed hard on the unforgiving earth. She'd seen an opening a few seconds ago, so she'd taken it. Blood loss or not, she wasn't letting Silus leave with Rue. She would have to be unconscious or dead for that to happen.

Something cracked. Her wrist?

Thank the stars for adrenaline. For the moment, the pain was negligible. So, she took advantage of the momentary reprieve and crawled on her knees and one good hand toward Silus and Sharon. She was putting up a good fight, but he was stronger and meaner.

Blaize dove over top of her, scoring a direct hit with Silus's midsection and one-arming him.

Sharon was now out of the way and stumbled a couple of steps to her left and then caught herself on the vehicle. She managed to stay on her feet.

Silus was a flurry of fists and kicks. The only reason he was landing any punches or kicks was because Blaize was in a weakened state. Carys had no doubt he would easily take care of Silus in a fair fight.

The amount of blood on Blaize's shirt was concerning. Plus, he'd been exerting himself. He was far from full strength.

Sharon dropped by her side, essentially blocking her from helping Blaize. "Where do you think you're going?"

Rosie turned. "We can lock the doors and call 911. Let's get inside the house."

"I'm not leaving him." Carys's tone must have been finite because Rosie shrugged before turning her attention toward Sharon.

"Hurry. Before he—"

"I'm staying right here, Rosie. These people took care of my girl. I'm not leaving them when they need me." The sincerity in Sharon's tone touched a nerve with Carys. And she appreciated Sharon not turning her back.

"I'm going," Rosie said.

"Do you what you need to do." Sharon reached for Carys's hand.

The woman bolted toward the house.

"Thank you," Sharon said, helping Carys to her feet. "Let's stop this guy together."

"Let's go!"

Blaize was holding his own, but when Carys saw an opportunity to slam the opened door into Silus's head, she took it.

He immediately went limp.

Blaize took the opportunity to roll the man over, forcing him face down while he hoisted Silus's hands behind his back.

Carys couldn't go any longer. "I need to sit."

That was all she could get out of her mouth before she plopped down, back against the vehicle, and then blacked out.

SIXTY SECONDS WAS all it took for everything to change. A flood of activity happened as law enforcement and EMTs roared up to the scene. But all Blaize could focus on was Carys, leaning with her back against the car, limp. Her eyes were closed, and from his position it looked like her breathing was shallow.

Fighting exhaustion, fatigue, and a wave of nausea so huge it threatened to bend him in two, he yelled for someone to take over so he could go to her. With every fiber of his being, he needed to see that she was alive.

The stress knot in his chest tightened as a deputy took over. Blaize rolled onto his back, needing to catch his breath and gather enough strength to stand up so he could walk to Carys.

"Sir, I need to examine you. Okay?" an EMT with the name *Andrew* sewn onto his pocket asked after coming into view.

Blaize shook his head as he forced himself to sit up. He saw stars. The world spun faster.

"Hey, let me help you," Andrew said. "I'll get you fixed up and feeling better in no time."

A stretcher was already being brought over by another EMT—Andrew's partner, no doubt.

Another worked on Carys, blocking his view.

Blaize craned his neck in an unproductive attempt to get eyes on her. He attempted to stand up, landed hard on his backside, and bit back a string of curses.

"Whoa, there," Andrew said, immediately jumping into action to keep Blaize from slamming his head on a tree trunk. "What are you trying to do?"

"Carys," he said, again vainly attempting to get a visual on her. "I need to know her status."

"I can check if you promise to sit tight." The EMT looked resigned.

"Promise."

Andrew studied Blaize for a long moment, like he was

deciding if he could trust the answer. "Okay. I'll be right back. Stay here."

"Got it."

He jogged over and took a knee next to the EMT working on Carys. It was all Blaize could do to stop himself from following. Out of the corner of his eye, he saw Silus regaining consciousness while being cuffed. A deputy was espousing Silus's rights, including the one to remain silent.

Silus spit dirt out of his mouth as he was hoisted up. He glared at Sharon, who stood a few feet away with Rue in her arms. Her attention was on Carys.

"You bitch," Silus ground out as the deputy led him away and toward the back of his SUV.

"Mind your language when you're speaking to a lady," the deputy said.

Silus scowled. He was going to be locked away for a very long time once all his crimes came to light.

Unfortunately, Sharon would face justice too. It was a shame the lengths she had to go to in order to feel safe from Silus. She'd protected her daughter, though, and Blaize would see to it Rue knew her mother.

Thinking clearly while he didn't know if Carys would live or die wasn't an option. He would figure the rest out later.

Andrew came jogging back. "I'll give you the update if you let me check out that arm of yours."

"That's blackmail."

"I know." He shot a look of apology. "It's also the only way I'll convince you to let me help."

"Fine." Blaize rolled up his shirt sleeve.

Andrew went to work as Carys was lifted onto the stretcher. A neck brace caught his attention. And, of course, the blood. There was so much blood.

Rosie had joined Sharon, both giving statements. From this distance, he heard Sharon admit to the sheriff she'd been the one to attack Carys's vehicle the other night, thinking she would scare her into running away from the car and leaving the baby. Sharon would then take her daughter and disappear. She'd made up the name Stephanie Cross, stitching together a new identity after learning she was pregnant. One that wouldn't raise flags for a life that didn't yet exist. If everyone believed Sharon was dead, no one would come looking for her after she grabbed her child and ran. The fiery crash had been a setup. Desperate, she'd taken advantage of a stranger's misfortune and accelerated the plan. The woman perished at some point overnight. Sharon had come across the deceased person on a park bench, and then seized the opportunity. It had all happened so fast. The moves had been meant to ensure Rue's safety. Sharon had also been the one to break into Carys's place to poke around.

"Can you hurry?" he asked, hearing the impatience in his own voice.

He winced as Andrew put pressure on the wound.

"Sorry about that," Andrew said, working his magic.

"It's fine." Blaize might have said the words, but if he lost Carys, nothing would ever be fine again. She needed to know how he felt.

Would he get the chance to tell her?

CARYS BLINKED HER eyes open. Her first thought? Blaize. Her second? Rue.

"Hey." Blaize's masculine voice sent ripples of awareness through her.

She exhaled. "You're here?"

"Right here," he said, squeezing her hand. It was then she realized he'd been holding it.

She was groggy and felt disconnected to her body until the warmth of his hand brought sensation back. "Where's Rue?"

"She's safe." He was quiet for a moment, then said, "Kit told me about the medication she needed, so Raiden picked it up. Thank you for asking her, by the way."

"I'm just happy that worked out." She reached for water with her free hand, her mouth was as dry as dirt in a draught and her tongue felt like sandpaper.

A few sips of water helped. Moving hurt like hell.

"I can get whatever you want," he said, studying her as she winced. "You don't have to move."

"Water's good," she said as she looked at him. *Really* looked at him. Dark circles cradled his eyes. Had he slept at all? "How long have I been out?"

"Thirty-seven hours and…" He checked his watch. "Forty-two minutes."

"I lost a whole day?"

"You've been in and out since surgery."

"Right." She had a vague memory of needing to remove bullet fragments out of her upper thigh. "What about Sharon?"

"She turned herself in this morning. She's been staying at the ranch, helping out. The sheriff said he would release her with an ankle bracelet until her court date since there was an abusive situation. We worked out a deal for her to keep an eye on Kit in exchange for room and board."

"That's a relief," she said. "It seems like you'll get the help you need while you focus on the ranch. That's great." Was this the end of the road for the two of them? Because her heart squeezed so hard she could barely breathe at the thought of losing him. "Everything is working out for the best."

"Not everything." He locked gazes with her and butterflies released in her stomach. "Carys, we've only known each other a short time, but it feels like so much longer. Like we met before in some alternate space and time and we're reconnecting now." He paused a beat. "I don't want you to feel any pressure, but I've fallen hard for you. I have never felt this deeply or connected to anyone else. What we have is special to me, and I don't want to lose you. I'm in love with you, Carys, heart and soul. And I would very much be honored if you would consider marrying me."

Carys's mouth dropped open.

"You don't have to decide today or anytime soon," he said when she couldn't formulate words adequate to express her emotions. Had he misread her? Because she loved this man. "I just wanted you to know how I feel. No, I needed you to know how I feel and what my intentions are." His thumb drew circles in her palm, and it was the most tender, most sensual act. "I can't imagine spending another day without you, but I'll wait until you're ready. I'd wait an eternity for you."

"You won't have to, Blaize," she said, finally able to find the words. "Because I'm head over heels in love with you. I think I was from the moment we met. It was like some deep-down part of me recognized you, and I've felt the pull ever since. The more I'm around you, the stronger the force. I love you, Blaize. And I want to do forever with you."

A hot tear streaked down her cheek. He thumbed it away.

"But there's one condition," she said. "And then you have my full heart and soul."

"Name it."

The fact that he didn't hesitate gave her hope.

"I want to be foster parents to Rue until Sharon gets out of trouble and back on her feet," she said.

"Already done," he said. A smile toyed with the corners

of those full, sexy lips. "Does that mean you'll put up with me for the rest of our lives?"

"You couldn't chase me away if you tried."

Carys had found the one place she felt like she belonged. She found her person.

"There's one more thing," he said after pressing a tender kiss to her lips.

"More surprises?"

"I hope this is a good one," he said, pushing up to standing.

She cocked her head to one side. "What are you up to, Blaize?"

"I tracked down your father. After being with Rue, seeing what a parent goes through, I decided he should know what happened to his daughter."

"And?" She didn't want to give away the sudden blossom of hope inside her that the relationship between her and her father could be reconciled.

"He dropped everything and drove here," Blaize said. "He's been sitting out in the hallway ever since. Do you want to see him?"

Those words sprouted wings in her soul.

"Yes," she said.

"Hold on." Blaize stepped to the door, cracked it open, and waved.

A few seconds later, her father walked into the room. His steps were tentative. His gaze unsure.

"Hi, Dad."

He broke down into tears. "My baby girl. I'm so sorry for the way I've treated you. But I've missed you every day since you walked out the front door with that beaten-up suitcase. Can you ever forgive me?"

Carys smiled through tears. "Already done, Dad. Come sit with me for a while."

The two most important men in Carys's life were right in front of her, so close she could reach out and touch them.

So, she did.

"Thank you for coming, Dad."

"This is long overdue, my girl," he said. "And I have a lot to make up for, if you'll let me."

"Everyone deserves a second chance if they're serious about making amends."

Blaize moved beside her and took her by the hand. In that moment, she knew she'd found home. And she planned to hang on to him for the rest of her life and whatever came next because if she lived a hundred lives, she would want every one of them to be with him.

* * * * *